Her need for him had to be denied..

As Joshua's mouth descended on hers, Christy was incapable of flight or fight. The maleness of him, the suffocating depth of his kiss, the overwhelming passion and power in that hard lean body— all combined to destroy her defenses.

Until reality returned, and she wrenched herself from his embrace. "How dare you!" she gasped. "You know we can't—"

"Christy, have you any idea what you do to me?"

"I know what *any* woman does to you!" she flung back.

Storm clouds gathered in Joshua's eyes. "Do you really think I'd take just *any* woman into my bed? You blind little fool— don't you know it's you I want?"

THE AUTHOR

Abra Taylor was born in India and has
lived in several exotic locales, but her
home for many years now has been
Canada. She combines writing with a
full-time career as a wife and as mother of
four children. While Ms Taylor has always
been a writer, romance fiction has become
her focus in the past few years.

Books by Abra Taylor

HARLEQUIN TEMPTATIONS
23—SUMMER SURRENDER

HARLEQUIN SUPERROMANCES
1—END OF INNOCENCE
5—CLOUD OVER PARADISE
12—A TASTE OF EDEN
21—RIVER OF DESIRE
38—A RAGE TO POSSESS

HARLEQUIN PRESENTS
342—LOST MOUNTAIN

These books may be available at your local bookseller.

For a list of all titles currently available,
send your name and address to:

Harlequin Reader Service
P.O. Box 52040, Phoenix, AZ 85072-2040
Canadian address: P.O. Box 2800, Postal Station A,
5170 Yonge St., Willowdale, Ont. M2N 5T5

Summer Surrender

ABRA TAYLOR

Harlequin Books

TORONTO • NEW YORK • LONDON
AMSTERDAM • PARIS • SYDNEY • HAMBURG
STOCKHOLM • ATHENS • TOKYO • MILAN

Published August 1984

ISBN 0-373-25123-8

Printed in Canada

1

IT WAS ONE of those cool summer days when a haze lies over the sun and the sea. It was not quite a fog; the visibility was reasonable. In the bright gray whiteness, Brant Point Lighthouse had loomed, and passed, and now been put behind. The ferryboat had rounded the point and the jetties, and beyond the sea of small craft that crowded the harbor lay the picture-postcard town of Nantucket. It, too, appeared all gray and white and touched with a soft light, perhaps because the shingled sides of nearly all the buildings were weathered by time and salt air to a soft silver color that no coat of paint could ever have achieved.

To Christy Sinclair, leaning over the rail of the ferryboat where she had spent much of the past hour trying to entice swooping gulls with the remaining crumbs of a sandwich lunch, it was a familiar enough scene. Nantucket was not her birthplace, but Cape Cod was. Although she had been working in Boston for some years, her parents still lived on the Cape, in the sprawling, much-added-to New England saltbox home where she and her brothers had been born. Catching the ferryboat to Nantucket or Martha's Vineyard was not the kind of thing you did every day, but more than once during childhood she had made the trip with her parents. Today the view of the island and the town gave her pleasure, as it always had.

Now the ferry was grunting, groaning, splashing and

backwatering as it tried to inch into its slip. The crowd waiting on the steamboat wharf was smaller than crowds Christy remembered from other summer visits. It was off-season, of course—still only mid-June, and the real tourist rush didn't start until July. No one would be waiting for her, she knew. She had been told to arrive at her own convenience, sometime before Saturday, and Saturday was still two days away. Only the fact that Christy's parents had left for a long-planned European holiday had brought her here early. The woman who had hired her, a Mrs. Cousins, had told her that the local taxicabs would know the way to Graydunes, and Christy had also been informed that there was a gardener on the grounds who would provide the front-door key. She had been instructed to use one of the bicycles in the garage—everyone bicycled on Nantucket—should she happen to arrive early. No, no one would be meeting her; but she was relieved, all the same, to see that several taxis were waiting nearby.

Men were shouting now and throwing ropes; others on the dock began to make the ferry fast. The sound of clanking chains told Christy that soon the gangplank would be lowered into position. A sudden freshening wind gusted across the deck, lifting skirts and promising clearer skies. Christy pushed her whipping brown hair out of her eyes and heaved at the suitcases beside her. Already the companionway leading down from the deck of the ferry was crowded with passengers waiting to disembark. It seemed she was the last person left on deck. Christy quickened her pace: it was impossible to tell how many others would be needing taxis today, and she did not want to miss getting a ride.

She had almost reached the companionway, suitcases underarm, when she remembered the head scarf she had removed earlier and tied to the ship's rail. She wheeled around to retrieve it.

"Oh!"

The shock and pain of the collision took her breath away and brought tears stinging to her eyes. She was hardly conscious of the fierce intake of pain that came from some other person, and the soft swearword that accompanied it, because there was another reason for Christy's distress—a reason that kept her, for the moment, from seeing who had been responsible for her predicament.

"Oh, *no!*" she agonized, her eyes riveted in dismay to the deck—and the contents of one suitcase that littered it. She dropped to all fours and started to scoop armloads of summer clothes back into the case.

The other person involved had as yet made no move to help her; but now, at last, he spoke.

"I'm sorry," said a voice deep but somehow strained. Christy glanced briefly upward to see a long lean length of gray tweed trouser and a white turtleneck sweater above it.

"Look what you've done," she accused, her eyes once more back on the deck and her scattered possessions. How could he stand there making no effort to help?

Belatedly the man dropped down beside her to lend a hand. "It takes two to collide," he returned in a polite voice that still sounded forced.

Christy paused in her task of gathering clothes and looked at the tall spare figure crouched beside her on the deck. Now, with his face down on a level closer to her own, Christy could see that the man, like the town beyond his shoulders, seemed almost silvery in appearance. His hair was ash blond, straight and too short to be whipped by the new breeze. His eyes, turned downward toward the deck, were not at the moment visible, but the lashes that hid them were pale, too, stubby and almost silver tipped. He was perhaps a dozen years older than she—past thirty-five, Christy guessed.

It was a compelling face, half sensual, half ascetic. Only gauntness saved it from being too handsome. The gauntness turned the face to all hard angles and taut skin over bone. Most remarkable was the mouth—a hard, finely chiseled mouth that at this moment was set into lines too grim to be prepossessing. Altogether unusual, decided Christy, noting a pallor in his complexion that made her wonder briefly if he spent most of his time indoors. But his lean body, though overly thin, appeared powerful and well coordinated beneath the cable-stitch sweater he wore. No, the man did not really look as though he spent most of his time behind a desk.

"Where did you come from?" she asked with growing curiosity. "I thought I was alone on deck."

"I was up top with the captain. He's an old friend." The man paused in his task, and his eyes came up to meet hers—deep-set gray eyes behind the thick blond lashes. For a moment Christy forgot to be annoyed, for the eyes had pain in them, a very real pain that was betrayed in no other way by his expression.

"It's my fault, too," she admitted, fighting a peculiar constriction in her throat. "Did I hurt you?"

"No." The eyes fell away from hers again, and the man set himself once more to picking up the scattered contents of a makeup case. "You must be moving in for the entire summer," he observed sardonically.

"I am. I have a summer job." She pounced on a box of stationery that was threatening to burst open and blow all over the deck.

"Mmm. A student," he remarked, and Christy did not for the moment enlighten him. She knew that her ragged pixie haircut and open-air complexion made her appear younger than her twenty-four years, especially when she was clad as she was now, in lean white corded trousers and a tightly ribbed red turtleneck sweater to combat the coolness of the sea air across the Sound. And today her scrubbed face bore little trace of makeup that might have made her appear her own age—only a touch of lipstick, and she was sure her lunch had made short work of that.

She was not a beautiful girl, but Christy had never minded that. She had been brought up with too much love and security to resent the fact that she seldom drew second glances, except when her face was transformed by a smile. She had a good figure, slender in the right places and reasonably endowed in others; a marvelous complexion; a warm generous mouth; and level wide-set hazel eyes that often danced with little golden lights. With these assets, she had found that her rather ordinary girl-next-door looks were no deterrent to dating in the tiny community where she had grown up. And for the past seven years there had always been David. David, who had first shown interest the year he left for medical school; David, whose ring she now wore; David, whom she would marry next year, when his internship at that reputable Baltimore hospital was finished. Not that she saw him as often as she would have liked, but he had always remained an anchor in her mind. Because of David, Christy had never taken time to doubt her ability to attract and hold a man.

"I thought your generation no longer bothered with these things," said the deep well-modulated voice beside her.

Christy looked up to see the stranger retrieving a wisp of black brassiere. His eyes now held mockery, not pain; and she felt her earlier annoyance flood back at the way the smoky gaze traveled downward from her neckline, causing a blush to move simultaneously upward.

"You were in an awful hurry a minute ago," she replied with more than a suggestion of sarcasm, snatching the undergarment from his hands. "Don't let me keep you."

"I was heading for my car," he informed her. "And yes—I will have to go now. The cars are starting to drive off the ferry."

Already he was rising to his feet, and Christy's eyes angrily followed the unfolding length of gray tweed trouser. Surely he must know that her suggestion had been pure sarcasm! Her possessions still lay scattered on the deck, some blown to a distance by the fresh wind.

"Are you just going to walk away and leave me with this mess?" The grievance in her voice was clear to hear.

"I'm afraid I have to." And it was true—already honking sounds from below deck advertised the fact that drivers in one of the lineups were impatient for him to arrive. "But I'll give you a lift somewhere, if I may. I'll wait for you onshore. It's the least I can do."

"I don't know exactly where I'm going," she returned without warmth. "I can't give you directions. I'll take a taxi."

"I know Nantucket rather well. Perhaps I can help you."

"No, thanks." She turned her face back to the deck, dismissing him. What was it about the man that irritated her? The damnable lean-boned handsomeness, perhaps; or the fact that he carried no luggage himself; or the fact that he drove a car on this island, where cars were the exception rather than the rule; or the fact that he had not admitted to the pain she had seen in his eyes; or perhaps just the mocking little smile that had been playing around his firm lips.

He hesitated a moment longer before leaving, and Christy did not even follow him with her eyes. But moments later, when she glanced upward to see a sleek silver gray Mercedes sports car purring its way onto dry land, she had no doubts as to who its driver might be.

Damn him anyway, she thought as she bounced on her old suitcase for the tenth time in an effort to make it close. But the now disarrayed clothes inside no longer allowed her to fasten the clasp, and it wasn't until a member of the ferryboat's crew came to her aid, some minutes later, that Christy was finally able to manage the feat.

By the time she found her way to the wharf, all the taxis had bumped off along the cobblestoned streets, and somehow that seemed the last straw. By now Christy was annoyed with herself, not the vanished stranger. Oh, why hadn't she accepted his offer of a ride! All because of some momentary irritation that had been childish and unreasoning—and quite out of character with the normally levelheaded person she knew herself to be.

In vexation she chewed at her lip for a few moments while she tried to decide what to do. At length she approached a member of the ferryboat crew who was still busily engaged on the dock.

"Can you tell me where to find a taxi?"

He scratched his head thoughtfully. "Bit late, aren't you?"

"Well, yes, I suppose I am. Do you know of a place called Graydunes? I could walk if it's not too far."

"Well, now—"

Suddenly the deckhand's face lit up, and he pointed to someone who was just now ambling onto the wharf. "Ask Old Tom—Tom Maybee. He'll help you."

Christy turned to see a wiry figure topped by a face

like old beaten leather and a shock of thick white hair.
"Thanks," she said, and hurried over to the newcomer.

"I beg your pardon," she began. "I'm looking for a
place called Graydunes. Do you know of it?"

"Ayeh," drawled the man in that soft, breathy New
England affirmative that turns one syllable into two,
and sometimes three.

"All the taxis have gone. I could walk, but I don't
know the way. I've been told you might help me."

The man scratched at a plaid-shirted arm, and pale
blue eyes blinked at her in slow motion. With gnarled
fingers he pulled a pack of cigarette tobacco from the
hip pocket of his shapeless trousers and home-rolled a
smoke before he answered, complacently and noncom-
mittally, "Mebbe." Then he put the cigarette into his
mouth, and although he located a wooden match, he
did not light it. "Ain't nobody goes to Graydunes."

"All the same, that's where I'm going. Do you know
the way?"

"Ayeh." But although Old Tom admitted to the
knowledge, he was not about to divulge it so easily. Instead he rubbed at his sandpaper chin and contemplated
Christy over the dangling cigarette.

"Can you give me directions?" she asked, more pointedly.

"Owner ain't there," he returned equably, without
answering her question. "Been three years since I
clapped eyes on him. He ain't home."

Christy smiled engagingly, without losing patience.
"All the same," she went on, "I'm expected. I'll be working there. A Mrs. Cousins hired me. I can show you her
letter if you like."

"Cousins." He seemed to roll the name over in his
mind, along with the cigarette on his tongue. "Cousins.
That ain't the owner's name."

"I know that," nodded Christy in agreement. "She's the housekeeper. She hired me to help with the little girl."

"Miz Cousins ain't arriving till Saturday," he drawled, belatedly admitting to some knowledge of the household arrangements at Graydunes. "An' I hear tell there's a proper nanny, too. You a proper nanny?" He eyed her casual attire critically, displaying open disbelief.

"No. Perhaps I'd better introduce myself," offered Christy, knowing from past experience with this type of New Englander that there were certain stages she must pass through. "I'm Christy Sinclair. I work with retarded children. The school where I've been employed has been closed down for lack of funds, and I've been hired to lend a hand with young Natalie Brent."

"Ayeh," returned Old Tom, still unconvinced.

"Just for the summer," she went on. "The arrangements were all rather last-minute, I know, but with Mrs. Brent's death, and with Mr. Brent—*Dr.* Brent, I mean—still in hospital, why, I don't suppose anyone gave much thought to the child's summer holiday until her school term was nearly over."

"Reg'lar housekeeper died in the fire, too," offered the Nantucketer, becoming somewhat less closemouthed.

"Yes, I know. It must be dreadful for the little girl. No wonder she's having trouble in school."

"Tyke's lucky she was in school," observed Old Tom. "If she'd been home at the time, she might have been killed like her ma—or near killed, like her pa. Bein' at that fancy school saved her life, an' that's sure."

"I really do need to get to Graydunes," said Christy hopefully, for she could see he was beginning to soften up a little.

"Ayeh," he returned, "I can see that."

"Is it very far?"

"Three miles, less a bit, out 'long the Dionis shore." He jerked a thumb over his shoulder, in the general direction of the afternoon sun, which was now struggling to break through. "Big estate. Name's spelled out in white stones. Can't miss it. House is all locked up, though, tight as a drum."

"I've been told the gardener will let me in." Christy heaved her suitcases up, not pleased to think of a three-mile walk, but relieved at last to know where she was going. "Thanks for your help, Mr. Maybee. I appreciate it."

"Be a dusty walk," he observed slowly, weighing her suitcases mentally with a dour expression on his face.

Christy smiled again, with a certain guarded optimism that he might actually be about to offer her a ride. "I'm used to walking. I was born on the Cape."

"Were you now?" For the first time, Old Tom's face broke out of its suspicious mold, revealing a set of ivory teeth that was something less than complete. "Well, well! Come along, then. Graydunes is where I live, for I'm the aforesaid gardener, an' I'm off to there now. Give you a ride in the Jeep."

Christy hid her glimmer of amusement under a polite smile of thanks. As Old Tom helped her carry her suitcases toward where the Jeep was parked, he became, at last, quite garrulous.

"Live over the garage, I do, in exchange for the grounds work. Or some of it—for my arthritis is pesky now, an' I'm not the man I was. Ain't much grounds, though—can't hardly mow a sand dune! An' that's what the property mostly is, down to the sea. Big stretch o' beach, an' even the cliff is no more'n a huge sand dune. One big lawn around the house. Rose gardens—best rose gardens this side of 'Sconset," he went on, and here a note of fierce proprietorial pride crept into his voice, "even if I do say so myself. Big house, built back in whaling days. But it's all shuttered up, dust cloths on everything. Miz Brent, when she was alive, she didn't hold with Nantucket *a*-tall. Had some fancy summer estate on Long Island—an' a penthouse in Noo York—an' the mansion in Connecticut, the one that burned down. Doc Josh, now, I used to figger he might hang his shingle up here, like his granddaddy did. Seems I was wrong."

"Doc Josh?"

"Dr. Joshua—Dr. Brent to you, I reckon, for you ain't known him since he was a tad, like I have. Born on Nantucket, Doc Josh was. But there ain't enough money here to hold a doc like him, leastways in winter. Not to compare with Fifth Avenoo. Rich ladies ain't about to travel this far fer a doc—no matter how good he is. No fancy big practice here!"

"Oh? Dr. Brent is a gynecologist—or an obstetrician?" asked Christy, who found herself beginning to dislike the fashionable Dr. Brent sight unseen.

"Ayeh. One of those fancy names. Doc fer the lady folk." They had reached the parked Jeep, and Old Tom loaded Christy's suitcases into the back seat, beside two bags of peat moss that were evidently the cause of his trip to town. He eased his creaking bones behind the wheel and waited for Christy to climb into place. "Makes a mint o' money at it, I shouldn't wonder. Though the family's allus had money—Doc Josh's great-great-great-granddaddy, now, he was a ship's owner an' made a fortune in whaling."

"Did he build Graydunes?"

The Jeep started to bump over cobblestones, a spine-jarring operation that seemed to bother Old Tom's arthritic bones not at all. "Ayeh, that he did. Near two centuries, Graydunes goes back. But it's all been done up real nice, not eight years since. Newfangled innards, stem to gudgeon. Not a penny spared! Only the best for Doc Josh. Yessiree! What's money to a man who rakes it in faster'n he can spend it? Near ripped the whole house apart an' put it back together again, piece by piece."

"It's a good thing the old architecture is valued around here," said Christy fervently, thinking that if it had not been for the local historical association, which prevented building out of character on the island, a man like "Doc Josh" sounded to be might have erected some modern monstrosity. Until today, if she had spared any thoughts for her hospitalized employer, she had thought of him with a certain amount of sympathy. "Have you heard how long Dr. Brent will have to remain in hospital?"

"All summer, as I hear tell. Plastic surgeons ain't through yet, for all that the fire was five months ago. Scarred something fearful, they say. Face all burned; chest, too. . . . Trapped by a burning timber, he was, an' the top half of him near charred to a crisp. An' at that, he's lucky. Fire truck arrived in time to save him, but not a soul else. Reckon he's a mite cut up about his wife, too. She was a looker. Ayeh. A real looker."

The story was a sobering one, and Christy was silent for a moment or two. By now the town had been left behind and the Jeep was moving slowly along an open country road. The brisk wind had continued to sweep the afternoon sky clean, and the world had changed from silver to a gently contoured palette of golds and browns and greens, with a blue sea beyond.

"And the little girl—it must be terrible for her," observed Christy.

"Can't say," said Old Tom. "Last time her pa brought her an' Miz Brent here, the tyke was but two years old.

After that he came back once or twice—but allus alone, an' only for a day or two. Never figgered the little one would turn out to be soft in the head, though. Big bright violet eyes an' black curls. Bound to be a looker—just like her ma."

"Perhaps part of the reason she's doing badly in school is her mother's death," Christy wondered out loud.

Old Tom shook his head in a firm negative. "Housekeeper that died, she was Nantucket born an' bred. Used to come back now an' then. Said the wee one couldn't learn simple letters, nor yet how to tie her shoes. Don't believe she's learned to read even yet. An' that was two, three years ago—when the child was but five."

Three years ago, then, thought Christy. Natalie Brent was eight now, or so Mrs. Cousins had told her. The child was now being sent to her third private school; the first two had considered her a hopeless case. What kind of parents would continue to inflict the torture of a regular school on a child who was unable to cope with the simplest task? Christy's heart twisted a little for the small girl whom she had not yet met.

"Did the parents ever think of sending her to a special school? It's not as though they couldn't afford it. There are others like the one I've been teaching at. A special school might have helped her."

"Miz Brent, from what I know, she wouldn't hear of it. Not a thing wrong with the girl, she said. Blamed the newfangled teaching methods for not drumming things into the wee one's head. Said no child o' hers could be retarded. No sir!"

"I see," murmured Christy without comment, but the thoughts in her head were not all kind.

Old Tom wheeled the Jeep into a long circular driveway lined with trees, and Christy noted the promised stones picking out the name Graydunes. From behind the trees a large spreading house came into view, silver shingled and white shuttered. It had a weathered gracious look that spoke of sea captains and other centuries. Part of its roof was squared off at the top, to form a flat surface above the slanting roof shingles, and that platform bore the railings that promised the existence of a widow's walk.

"Oh, how charming," breathed Christy with a warm rush of pleasure. "And those pink roses—why, Mr. Maybee, you've trained them to climb all over the sides! They're beautiful."

Although her companion didn't crack a smile at the compliment, Christy could practically feel his scrawny chest puffing out with pride. "Call me Old Tom. Everybody does," he ventured instead, almost offhandedly, and Christy felt as if he had offered her a compliment in return.

"Only new part is the garage," Old Tom pointed out, "an' it's been built to look as old as the rest. Room for four cars, an' very comfy quarters above, if I do say so." He pulled the Jeep up in front of wide steps and jerked on the hand brake. "Can't say the same for the big house right now. Miz Cousins laid on for some of the local ladies to come tomorrow an' take the dustcovers off, an' clean up a bit. Men coming to open the shutters, too. Used to do it myself, but with the arthritis I ain't the man I was. Till tomorrow, you'll have to make do."

"I'll manage," said Christy cheerfully enough. "All I need is one of the bikes from the garage—I hear you have several. I'll need to fetch some food from town before the stores close. I don't suppose there's any in the house."

"Not a morsel. Truth is, I'd offer to feed you, but I ain't much of a hand in the kitchen, an' I'm off to my sister's for supper. Don't keep much in stock—beans an' bacon is about it, so you'd best go back in town. Could drive you in, though."

"No, thanks. I'll take a bike. I might decide to eat in town."

"Spare Chevy in the garage," Old Tom told her.

"I've let my driver's license lapse, unfortunately. The bike will do me fine—and so will the exercise."

With a key fished from his pocket, Old Tom opened the front door and ushered Christy into the shuttered house. Surprisingly, it was not too dark inside. A skylight spilled sunshine over a broad circular staircase, lending an impression of air and light to the lower hall. A large living room to the right lay mostly in shadow. Dustcovers were everywhere, but an expanse of deep broadloom, with occasional Oriental prayer rugs, suggested that the furnishings would be luxurious indeed.

"Here, I'll help you up with these cases." Christy's escort started up the staircase. At its head, corridors branched in two directions, and here he halted. "Pick any bedroom you want—'cept the ones at that end." He pointed down one corridor. "That's Doc Josh's wing. His room at the far end. Miz Natalie's room right beside it. Then the nanny's room, first door this side—it goes through to Miz Natalie's room. Across the hall, Miz Brent's rooms. Nobody allowed in there, no sirree! All fixed up special, they were, according to Miz Brent's likes. Ain't the same as the rest of the house. Big hullabaloo to get it right, yet Miz Brent never used those rooms but twice."

He picked up the suitcase again and trudged along the hall that ran in the opposite direction. "Six bedrooms here. All real nice, an' all with their own bathrooms. Have to turn on the water for you, though—I'll do that from below stairs, before I leave. Well, now, take your pick."

"Anything will do." Christy opened the first of several doors and flicked on the wall switch, for the still-shuttered window allowed little light through, and here the skylight had no effect.

Old Tom put the suitcase down on a carpet the color of antique gold. The walls, papered in something that looked like an old Williamsburg pattern, repeated the tone. Christy moved about the room, pulling off dust-covers to reveal some very handsome Early American furniture—a spool bed with a quilt spread, a Shaker chest of drawers, a Boston rocker, other pieces equally simple and comfortable. "I'll be perfectly happy in this room," she remarked with a sense of genuine delight.

"Well, then." Old Tom shifted from one foot to the other and then moved toward the door. "I'll be off, if it's all the same to you, for I'm due to visit my sister over Madaket way. The bed's made up. Doc Josh allus said keep the house ready, in case. Sheets might be a mite musty, but they'll do for tonight, I reckon. Anything else you need?"

"Nothing else—but don't forget to turn the water on, will you? I'd like to wash up before I go back into town."

"Nice to see the old house used again," said Tom a little wistfully, with his gnarled hands on the doorknob. "Ayeh...real nice."

And then he was gone, closing the door behind him. The carpeted hallway muffled his retreating steps. Christy opened her suitcases and spent several minutes hanging up clothes, noting ruefully that many of the contents of the suitcase that had burst open would now need to be pressed; then several minutes putting other things into drawers. By the time she moved into the bathroom to inspect it, she could hear, faintly, the sound of water running elsewhere in the plumbing system. So Old Tom had remembered. Gratefully she turned the tap, and after a snort or two to protest long disuse, water gushed forth.

It took only a minute to wash up, and then she was back in the bedroom, stripping off her sweater. It was warm on the island, much warmer than it had been across Nantucket Sound, but that was only to be expected. She unearthed a blue-and-white-striped T-shirt that had escaped too much crushing and slipped it on without changing out of the white cords, which would be practical enough for a bike ride into town. A quick application of lipstick and a brush through her hair and she was ready to go. She slung her handbag over one shoulder and headed along the corridor to the staircase.

On impulse she halted at the head of the stairs. Several things Old Tom Maybee had said had made Christy curious to know more about the mother of the girl she would be teaching. What kind of a woman had Mrs. Brent been? Perhaps those rooms, decorated to her taste, would provide some clues. And what better chance to see them than right now? After today there would be other people constantly around the house. Tomorrow a troop of local women would arrive, as she had been told; the following day would bring the housekeeper and the nanny and the child.

Following the impulse without a single twinge of conscience, for she felt her motives were quite respectable, Christy turned toward the forbidden suite of rooms that had been Mrs. Brent's. She opened the door and her hand felt for the light switch.

She was curiously disappointed. Inside everything seemed cold and white—an effect due in part to the white dustcovers over everything, Christy realized. This was a sitting room; there was no bed. Several oversize avant-garde paintings hung on the pale oyster-toned walls, and these, although they lent great swoops of dramatic color to the otherwise barren room, seemed to Christy to have little warmth or meaning, although she was not particularly antagonistic to some modern art. Peeking beneath the dustcovers only confirmed her reservations about the room. There seemed to be a great deal of chrome and glass, and a considerable amount of white leather and black suede, with only discreet touches of color. Everything was in the best possible taste. And yet . . . and yet it was the kind of room put together by expensive decorators, a room that was restrained and elegant and perfect, a room with no particular personality stamped on it.

A door led into a large and luxurious bedroom that offered very little improvement, to Christy's way of thinking. Here the furniture was Oriental in design, lacquered lipstick red, and the walls were covered with a dramatic yellow watered silk. Strangely, despite the wealth of color in this room, it seemed to have no more warmth of individuality than its black-and-white neighbor.

There was an adjoining dressing room—empty. Nothing hanging there to suggest what its owner might have been like. And a bathroom: all white plush carpeting with black fixtures and a sunken tub. Gold taps like swans' heads were the only touch of eccentricity in an otherwise characterless room. Nothing, nothing, nothing—nothing but money, thought Christy. How preferable was the cozy room in which she herself was installed! What kind of a woman, and mother, had Mrs. Brent been? So far these rooms had revealed nothing.

But there was yet another door, at the far end of the bedroom. Christy reached it, turned the knob, pushed it open. And froze.

"Good *God!*" said an astonished male voice.

But if the man was shocked, so was Christy—so shocked it took her several moments to realize who this was, standing tall and completely naked across the room.

At the moment of her advent the man had frozen like a jungle animal on alert, his muscles totally tensed yet totally still. His face and upper torso were in semidarkness, but the pool of light that fell from a single bedside lamp clearly illuminated the lower half of his body, and it was this that Christy saw first. The sight burned itself into her brain in several short seconds that seemed to last a small eternity.

His stance was such that he directly faced the door, where she stood. He remained briefly motionless, feet planted slightly apart, the thews of his calves stilled yet elastic with readiness. No tendons moved in his long athletic legs, but the contained power that emanated across the room suggested the strength of a coiled spring. No muscles rippled visibly beneath the firm skin of his lean flanks, but their underlying tautness could be sensed. He was extremely spare and sinewy, magnificently male, his unsunned body pale and hard as marble.

The unexpected sight of a man's nakedness, overwhelming in virility, did peculiar things to Christy's core. Strange little quivers started to assault her, as if a thousand sleeping butterflies began to waken and tremble in her limbs. For a few vital moments she felt incapable of movement, incapable even of lifting her eyes to seek a safer part of his anatomy. She simply stared, shocked.

He had been toweling his hair, and now, recovering more swiftly than Christy, he lowered the towel with what appeared to be an unbecoming lack of haste. He hitched it over his lean hipbones, tucking a fold into place over the rock-firm flat of a stomach covered by a light downward drift of crisp ashen body hair. The movement jerked Christy back to sanity. No longer mesmerized by the statue-still vision of virility, her widened eyes lifted higher.

Without a word she pulled the door closed between them and felt her pulse start operating again, triple time, like a jackhammer. Of course it had to be *him*. How many men had such gaunt height, such leanly fleshed muscularity, such extraordinary ash blond hair?

Before she had time to beat a retreat the door was yanked open and she was confronted with the full fury of a scowl that told her this was a man with one overriding emotion at the moment: anger.

"What the hell are you doing here?"

Her eyes boggled at him and then escaped to the relative safety of yellow silk walls. She could not yet speak. She was too overcome by the impropriety of the situation she had stumbled into so unwittingly and by the shock of what she had just seen...of *whom* she had just seen. Although she could not look at him directly now, she could still see every detail of him in her mind's eye. The sight of his sinewy nakedness was not the only thing imprinted on her brain. Her memory saw other things, too—the straight crisp hair he had been toweling, still ashen pale but shades darker from the shower; the gray eyes, now glittering and dangerously stormy; the firmly molded, sensuously shaped mouth; the strong hands with their long sensitive fingers.

And the scars. Across his chest and one muscled shoulder had been a wide ugly band of reddened flesh, barely healed from severe burns. The scars had not been readily visible when his upper torso had been in shadow, but in the light of the doorway they had been startlingly evident.

"I asked a question. Who the hell are you, and what d'you think you're doing in my wife's bedroom?"

"I...I'm Christy Sinclair." She managed to croak the words out in an unnatural voice.

"Is the name supposed to mean something to me?" His voice was icy with sarcasm. "It doesn't explain your presence in my house—or in my wife's room."

She cleared her throat, restoring her voice to some semblance of normality. "I...I'm to work here. I thought I was alone in the house. I'm sorry; it was an unforgivable—"

Brutally, he broke through her nervous excuses. "You mean I've *hired* you? Good God!"

"Yes...well, it does seem that way, although I thought I'd be working under Mrs. Cousins. I heard you were to be in hospital for most of the summer. I didn't expect you to be here."

"Didn't you now," came the frosty reply. Christy became aware of his hands readjusting the white towel to a more secure position. "What you expected has nothing to do with it. I don't like the hired help prying through my wife's rooms—or mine."

"I wouldn't have gone through *yours*," she protested hotly, even though she knew her words would not be believed. "Please—I'm sorry; I don't know what to say. I feel terrible."

"Didn't it occur to you that my wife's apartment might connect with mine?" he said dryly. "Where did you think this door led?"

"I didn't think at all," she admitted. "And of course I didn't think you were here. If I had known that was *you* on the ferry—"

"Well, start thinking," he broke in. "About where

you can get another summer job. Now get out. Out of this room—and out of this house."

Her eyes flew to his face in alarm, but it was clear from the determined set of his gaunt jaw and the tight line about his mouth that he meant what he had said. His eyes were remote, like silver ice, suggesting that he was not a man who could be easily swayed. Nevertheless, she made an effort to protest.

"You can't mean that!"

"I can and I do. You're fired. Now!"

Christy swallowed. She longed not to humble herself. But she needed this summer job, for she and David were saving for the down payment on a house; and since David earned almost nothing during his long internship, he had been able to contribute very little. Soon, too, David would have the expense of setting up a practice. The fact that she no longer had a job for the fall further complicated matters. When Christy had first heard of this position, her special qualifications had allowed her to ask Mrs. Cousins for a very generous salary, and get it. But then, not many employers wanted those special qualifications, and she knew it might be impossible to find another summer position calling for her exact experience with retarded children.

"Please give me another chance. I assure you I don't normally do this kind of thing." Now, fighting to keep her job, she felt curiously calmer. Even the sight of that lean, autocratic, disapproving face looming over her could no longer drive her eyes away, and she met his gaze levelly. "It was something Mr. Maybee—Old Tom—said. About your wife's rooms being decorated especially to her tastes. I thought if I could learn a little about the mother, it would help me to understand."

Some of the anger in his eyes was displaced by puzzle-

ment. "What do you mean? What is there to understand?"

"The child—*your* child, that is. Retarded children
have feelings, too. She's sure to be upset about her
mother's death. It helps to understand the back-
ground—gives a foundation to work on. And I didn't
expect you'd be around to answer any of my questions."

Clearly he was totally confused. A frown tugged at
his brow and narrowed his hard eyes. "I thought you
were a student—a live-in maid, perhaps. What were
you hired for? Surely you're not the nanny? I thought
you'd be arriving with Natalie."

"No, I'm the teacher."

"You don't look old enough—I heard you'd had a few
years' experience."

"I'm twenty-four, and I've been working with retarded children for three years."

"Oh, Lord." He ran his fingers through his pale short
hair and looked at her with a rapidly changing expression.

Christy could see something almost like apology in
his face, and tried a guarded smile. "It was wrong of me,
I know. But Old Tom told me nobody was allowed in
here, and I thought Mrs. Cousins might refuse to let me
see through later. I wouldn't have pried in your room.
Honestly."

At last he seemed to believe her, and his voice when
he spoke again had lost all of its antagonism. "I take
back what I said. Of course you're not fired. I'm glad
you didn't just walk out of here! Mrs. Cousins had a
hard enough time finding someone with experience. I
think she wrote to every special school within a
thousand-mile radius."

"Didn't she tell you my name?"

"Possibly—but there were so many arrangements to

be made, so many details I couldn't look after myself. I'm afraid I've been in a convalescent home between operations. You'll have to forgive me."

"I thought you were still in hospital," she ventured.

"I was due to go back in today. More skin grafts." He gestured at his chest, and Christy let her eyes slide downward, then averted them with a swift embarrassment she did not manage to hide.

He gave a short bitter laugh and said cynically, "Not very pretty, is it?"

"It's not the scars, it's...." But how could she tell him it was the memory of his earlier nakedness? She forced her eyes to travel back to his spare frame. With the evidence of square well-muscled shoulders before her eyes, it was easy to see he had lost weight during his recent illness, although perhaps not as much as his thinness suggested. The skin lay taut over his bones and had none of the slackness that excessive weight loss would cause. All the same, his ribs were quite countable, and across his flat abdomen there was evidence only of corded muscle—none of flesh. From the wide band of angry scar tissue that ran across his body—from one side of his rib cage diagonally upward to his other shoulder—it was plain to see in what manner he had been trapped by a burning timber. There were other, smaller scars, too, many others, but these had already started to fade and in places were partially concealed by a new growth of crisp pale hair on his chest.

"Agh, Miss, er, Sinclair. You don't need to pretend. I know it's hideous." He sounded impatient; whatever emotion he had seen in her eyes, he must have mistaken it for horror. "I can see you're wondering why I didn't let the plastic surgeons finish the job they started. I know I have all the appeal of raw liver right now! But I decided the medical profession could wait and my daughter couldn't. It was a sudden decision on my part to come here and surprise her—a decision the doctors weren't quite in accord with, I'm afraid. I checked myself out of the convalescent home late last night and drove up to the Cape. I managed to get a berth for my car on the Woods Hole ferry—you know the rest. I wanted to be waiting here when my daughter arrived."

Christy wrenched her eyes away from his torso and directed them to more neutral regions, somewhere around his chin. She was unaccountably disturbed, but not by the scars. "I did hurt you, then, when we collided. You should have told me."

"I'm still in one piece, aren't I? Even if it's not a very pretty piece." He ran one hand around the back of his neck, wearily, a gesture of resignation. Christy noted that his fingers, like the rest of his body, were long and lean and hard—strong fingers, tapered and competent, that suggested he would be a skilled doctor indeed. Her eyes traveled back upward to connect with his face as he added bitterly, "Yes, Miss Sinclair, the face, too. The bones are all mine, but it needed quite a bit of surface work, and in the process they managed to remove some nasty frown lines from my forehead. Another miracle of modern science. Now if you'll excuse me, I'm not used to being on my feet for so long, and—"

"Have you eaten anything today?" Christy interrupted with alarm, noting the deathly pallor of his lips and realizing he must have driven four hundred miles or more since the previous night.

He registered some surprise at her concern. "I'm too damn tired to be very hungry right now. But if you can bring me a black coffee I'd appreciate it."

"Black coffee isn't what you need," she told him firmly. "In any case, I haven't any, and your gardener told me there's nothing in the house. And he's gone off to visit his sister, so I can't get any from him. I'm going into town now to get some food. I'll get enough for you, too."

He smiled without humor, as though it were an effort. "What is this—a role change? I'm the doctor."

"And like most doctors I suspect you're a very bad patient. Can I help you to your bed?"

He shook his head, and the stubby blond lashes blinked at her. "No. But you're right about the other. I do need some food." He retreated a few steps, to the other side of the dividing door, and leaned heavily on the knob. "Anything. An egg...or just cheese and crackers will do."

"I won't be long," said Christy, backing slowly across the bedroom that had once belonged to this man's wife.

"And next time," he concluded in an oddly thin voice, "next time don't come through this way. My room is the last along the corridor."

He closed the door between them, and Christy turned and left, wondering if it was only his state of undress that made her feel like an awkward seventeen-year-old all over again.

2

A FLUFFY CHEESE OMELET, freshly squeezed orange juice, buttered toast, milk—it looked like a breakfast tray, Christy conceded, but the food had been chosen for ease and speed, and because she knew absolutely nothing about her new employer's likes and dislikes. He had mentioned eggs and cheese, so eggs and cheese it was.

Earlier—many hours earlier, immediately after returning from her bicycle trip to town—she had familiarized herself with the large friendly kitchen and prepared the exact same menu. But even loud knocking at the upstairs door had not aroused the owner of the house. After some hesitation, and with guilty memories of her earlier trespassing, she had turned the knob and looked inside. A lamp still burned beside Dr. Brent's bed, and it was clear to see he was in deep sleep. After sparing a swift appreciative glance for the room—earlier she had been too distraught to notice that its furnishings were similar to those in her own room, if somewhat more elegant—she had closed the door quietly behind her. Then she had retreated to her own room and eaten the first omelet herself. Since then she had listened occasionally, from the corridor outside his door, for sounds of wakefulness. She had detected none.

About nine-thirty Christy had heard the rumble and rattle of the returning Jeep; Old Tom had long since retired to his apartment over the garage. Two more hours had come and gone, and Christy, who was an early riser, had been fighting exhaustion. By then nearly eight hours had passed since her encounter with Dr. Joshua Brent. Surely he would be rested now? She could hardly go to bed without providing the promised food, but she had begun to regret her choice of eggs, which were never appetizing if allowed to sit. At last, with midnight only half an hour away, she had repeated her efforts in the kitchen, and it was this second tray that was now precariously balanced on one arm as she knocked once more at her employer's bedroom door.

It took several tries, but at last the response came in a voice thick with sleep. At his bidding, she opened the door with some difficulty and entered.

His gaze followed her approach across the room, but no smile. Although the rest had improved his color somewhat, he still looked exhausted, his eyes heavy lidded with sleep. Christy set the tray on a bedside table and smiled in a way that warmed her face.

"You'll have to sit up to eat this," she told him.

"Later—I'll eat it later." His voice sounded half-drugged, as though he were only waiting for her departure to return to his slumbers. "Thanks for bringing it."

"It won't keep. And you've had plenty of sleep—eight hours to be exact. You can rest again after eating."

He struggled to lift his arm out from under the covers and looked at his watch, then winced. "I thought you said you wouldn't be long."

"I did bring something earlier, but I couldn't wake you up. You *must* eat this time, for I won't make a third omelet, and I'm quite tired myself."

"Oh, God, a mother hen," he groaned, and pulled himself up in bed enough that Christy could see he was now decently clad in a pair of black silk pajamas. "Well, I'll eat it immediately, on one condition. Did you buy coffee?"

"Yes."

"Then go and make me a cup.

"Coffee will only keep you awake. How about tea?"

"Coffee."

"Tea."

"Coffee!"

"Hot milk?"

He frowned at her unhappily, obviously not content to be at her mercy. "All right, tea. At least it's hot. Good Lord, you're a stubborn bitch! Do you treat your children like this, too?"

"Sometimes," she admitted cheerily, and departed once more for the kitchen, this time leaving his bedroom door open behind her. Balancing trays and opening doors simultaneously was not a task she wanted to repeat.

By the time she returned, some minutes later, he was dozing again—this time in a half-sitting position with his pillow plumped against the gleaming mahogany head of the large antique sleigh bed. With sleep smoothing the frown from his face, he looked somewhat younger and less overwhelming—and again she was drawn by the chiseled line of his mouth, the way the shadows fell in bruised hollows around his eyes and below his cheekbones.

Christy noted with satisfaction that the omelet had been demolished, and some of the toast and the orange juice. But the milk...*where* was the milk glass?

With alarm she saw; and hastily put down the tea tray. He had dozed off with the milk glass, still quarter full, balanced on the far side of the large double bed, against an unused pillow. Carefully she leaned across to retrieve it, for it appeared that his hand might knock it over at any moment.

"Oh...!"

At the light touch of a hand on her breast, she nearly knocked the glass flying herself. Startled, she turned her face to his and saw that his eyes had come open. There was something naked and aching in those eyes—not the kind of pain she had witnessed on the boat, but very near it. His hand still rested lightly on her breast, and for reasons she did not care to analyze at that moment, she felt incapable of moving away. For a moment frozen in time, neither moved.

Then he groaned, a groan that seemed to come out of his very depths. His other hand slid upward to curl around her neck, his long hard fingers disruptively tender as they stroked her nape and threaded into her hair. For causes unknown she felt unable to stop him, to do anything but submit, as if in a dream.

Perhaps it was the raw hunger in his eyes that deprived her of reason, perhaps it was the sensuous magnetism exerted by his unsmiling mouth, perhaps it was the erotic surprise of his fingers trembling at her breast. He pulled her face slowly down to his. In a trance, she allowed it. For some moments he did no more than move his lips against hers with aching slowness, a gentle explorative touch that was not even a kiss. His mouth was lightly parted and so was hers. Her lips tasted the good male moisture of him; her nostrils swirled with the clean male tang of him; her skin stung with the hard male texture of him. His far-reaching fingers had started to gentle her earlobe, stroking it until a multitude of tiny nerve endings quivered into being.

His hand at her breast moved, too. Through the light T-shirt he had started to stimulate the nipple, molding and manipulating it between thumb and forefinger until it sprang into traitorous hardness, causing a sweet shock of sensation that further contributed to her inability to protest.

Unthinkingly she placed her hands against the surface of his thin black pajamas and felt the outer curve of his broad shoulders, warm and muscled and utterly masculine beneath the sliding silk. Her unruly wanton thoughts slipped to sensuous visions of what lay beneath the pajamas—the whip-lean length, the coiled reflexes, the taut marble flesh with its ashen dusting of disturbing texture she had found so strangely and excitingly erotic. The afterimage of his powerful maleness assaulted her, the intimate memory causing her mind to wheel and whirl.

Reacting to the aphrodisiacs of her senses and of her imagination, for one magical moment she gave in to urges as old as time. Hovering lightly above him, with parted mouth brushing feverishly against his, she closed her eyes and moaned.

Her soft moan was like a trigger. Taking advantage of the temporary softening of her lips, his tongue at once became a hard, probing, passionate weapon, driving deeply and demandingly into the vulnerable hidden cavern of her mouth. His fingers at her nape firmed their grip, capturing her forcefully, becoming at once imperative in molding her mouth closer against his own, fitting the open cavity more tightly against his own.

She could hear the hungry groaning deep in his throat, could feel the thud of his heart and the hot breath expelling at her cheek. For one mindless moment his unbridled ardor sent shooting stars of exhilaration exploding through her veins, and her mouth yielded to his passionate claim.

Her response did not last long, but it was all the encouragement he needed. He rolled in the bed, assuming the position of male aggressor. In one frenzied movement, while she was too startled to fight back, she found herself swept flat on the bed beside him. Her breath was half knocked from her lungs; her mouth was stifled by sudden shock and by the suffocating intrusiveness of the kiss that now drove her head against the pillow. Commanding her from above, his hands freed to roam at will, he searched her body with blazing urgency. His long fingers settled possessively over the full soft curve of her breast, while his palm moved in swift urgent little circles, as if he had become unbearably aroused by the feel of her thrusting hardened nipple.

Christy felt unbearably aroused, too. But then she remembered who he was and who she was, and she wrenched her head to one side. "Stop," she cried. "Stop!"

His mouth burned a predatory path to the edge of her lip, seeking to renew the interrupted kiss. His fingers tangled urgently in her hair with a strength and ferocity surprising in a man so recently ill.

Panic pounded through her veins. Or was it panic? It was fire and ice and a whole range of sensations she could not allow herself to feel with a man she hardly knew.

"Let me go!" she gasped. She started to struggle in earnest, flailing at his chest with her fists, uncaring that she might injure his still healing skin. She was thinking not of his burns but of his dangerous maleness, of her vulnerability, of their aloneness in that large and remotely situated house. "Let me go!"

He only tightened his grip. He shifted, his chest moving to pin her hands in place between them. His arms became girders of steel encircling her, effectively ending her battering resistance. She could feel the wall of him weighing on her breasts, could feel the tenseness of tightened tendons in his forearms, the pressure of his mouth against her throat. "I need you," he muttered hoarsely in a voice thickened by desire. His face burrowed into her hair, drinking in the fragrance of her, thirsting for her. "Oh, God, I need you. Don't fight me. If you only knew...."

But the torn plea might have been in Christy's imagination, for in the next moment he had rolled away. She sprang from the bed at once, clothing and senses in total disorder. She started to race for the door, yanking down her twisted T-shirt as she went.

"I apologize."

The swift stiffly spoken words stopped her when she had moved no more than a few steps, and she whirled around to glare at Joshua Brent, intending to lash at him with angry words. His eyes were shut, his face closed and wooden, his mouth austere. Only a single pulse throbbing in his temple betrayed emotion of any kind. It was as though the scene just played might never have happened. How could he wear a look of such asceticism after having behaved like a hot-blooded tomcat only moments earlier?

The change in him was so complete Christy's verbal attack was less poisonous than planned. "You shouldn't have done that," she choked out.

His lids feathered open, revealing gray depths that betrayed no warmth, no passion, no emotion. Something flickered in them, but it was only resentment— and perhaps pain. It was then that she remembered the burns. They had been raw, too newly healed for the kind of punishment she had inflicted. How badly had she hurt him with the wild drumming of her hands on his chest?

"Forgive me," he said stiffly. "It was a momentary lapse—an impulse."

"Impulse is no excuse," she said, but her voice was not as accusatory as it might have been. She took a tentative step toward the bed, her eyes drifting toward his pajama front, a frown of concern creasing her brow.

His eyes turned cold and shuttered, closing out pity. His mouth became hard, its chiseled lines deliberately cruel. "If you don't want to be kissed," he sliced at her with infuriating arrogance, "please don't dangle yourself within reach."

Christy felt as if she had been slapped. Sympathy vanished as her head jerked back to a defiant angle. How dared he imply that that whole scene had been her fault!

Anger at him—and perhaps at her own remembered weakness—sent color raging into her cheeks. The denials tumbled to her lips. "I wasn't doing anything of the kind. The milk—" she gestured furiously "—I was reaching for the milk."

Miraculously, it had survived, although it was now tilted at a precarious angle against the far pillow. He turned and saw, and restored the glass to safety. When he spoke again he had resumed politeness. "Look, Miss Sinclair, I'm sorry I implied it was your fault."

But Christy had not yet finished venting her annoyance. She broke through his words. "Do you always force yourself on women as you did just now? It must have been obvious to you that I was totally unwilling!"

"Not as obvious at first as it is now," he said in a dry voice. "At first I thought I detected some acquiescence—perhaps even response."

"You were wrong. The only response at first was shock—total shock that you would try such a thing!"

"Surely I'm not the first man who's laid a hand on you? You aren't exactly undesirable."

"But you are!" she flashed at him, and then immediately regretted it when she saw the way he frowned, and the way his hand traveled to the pajama top that covered his scarred flesh.

"I'm sorry; I didn't mean that," Christy denied quickly. "At least—"

"For God's sake, don't apologize," he said roughly. "You can't help your reaction. I was quite aware of it earlier."

"I didn't mean you were unattractive." Christy swallowed. How difficult this was, to explain to him that her thoughtless words an instant ago had been merely a defensive gesture on her own part; that they had borne no relation to his scars. Whatever she said, he was sure to disbelieve her.

"I only meant that you have no particular appeal for *me*, Dr. Brent." Good Lord, that hardly sounded better, thought Christy. She seemed to get in deeper with every word, and she did not dare admit to him that she was in fact attracted to him, far too much for safety. "It's not *you*—it's me. I'm engaged."

His eyes, cold and dispassionate, moved to her ring finger and found the square-cut diamond set in platinum. "So I see," he said sardonically. Where had it gone, all that intensity and passion of moments ago? If there was any emotion in his voice, it was a faint trace of scorn. "The ring doesn't suit you. He should have chosen something quite different."

"He had no choice in the matter." Christy was desperate to return the conversation to normality, and perhaps that was why she now offered more information than she might otherwise have done. "This was his mother's ring. Both David's parents are dead, and as he's still interning, and had to put himself through medical school, he hasn't the money to buy another."

His eyebrows tilted upward. With that part of herself that kept reacting to this man's compelling virility, Christy noted that they were a shade darker than the ash blond of his hair. "Then you're engaged to a doctor?"

"Yes."

"So you're to be a doctor's wife. How nice for you."

His voice was heavy with sarcasm, and Christy reacted. "I'm not marrying a medical degree, Dr. Brent, I'm marrying a man—the man I happen to love. I see nothing special in being a doctor's wife."

He grimaced and had the grace to apologize. "Look, I didn't mean my sarcasm that way. I wasn't talking about the social-status thing, which nowadays doesn't count for much. I just meant it's not the easiest life for a woman. A doctor often has to work long hours, go on calls in the middle of the night. It requires a certain amount of trust."

"Any marriage requires a certain amount of trust," responded Christy, still feeling vaguely hostile, even though she recognized the hostility as a defense mechanism. "Are you telling me it will be harder to trust David because he's a doctor? Maybe you know something about doctors that I don't know."

Now he, too, began to look exasperated. "I know something about human nature, and I expect you're no more perfect than any other woman. It's easy to mistrust a man who isn't in bed beside you."

"I happen to trust David," Christy said—and somewhere in the back of her mind she stored the thought that perhaps Dr. Joshua Brent's wife had not trusted him. For good reason?

She felt herself being dissected under a penetrating gaze. "Maybe you'll change your mind," he told her, "the first time he has to go out on a call at three in the morning."

"David won't have to. His specialty doesn't have that kind of emergency."

"What's his field?"

"Foot troubles—podiatry. He chose it for its regular hours."

Now those blond eyebrows were drawn together in disapproval, describing new frown lines, although he said nothing. Sensing his disapprobation, Christy asked, "Surely you're not finding fault with David's choice?"

"Of course not. The medical profession needs all kinds. But there are other reasons for choosing a specialty—interest, for one."

"Like *your* specialty?" she asked rather waspishly, for she felt that some defense of David was required. "Women, as I recall."

The response that cracked back at her was no more friendly than her own. "Obstetrics. Mainly *pregnant* women, Miss Sinclair. I happen to like delivering babies."

Christy began to feel remorse for her moment of chagrin. Why did Dr. Joshua Brent affect her this way, causing her to run through a month's gamut of emotions in a matter of minutes? Perhaps it was exhaustion. She was still standing on her feet, at the bedside of a man she had known for mere hours, at a time when she would normally be fast asleep. And yet she had to admit to herself that she did not really feel tired. On the contrary, she felt wakeful and alive in every tingling inch.

"But then," Dr. Brent was going on, and touches of humor had appeared at the edges of his mouth, "perhaps your fiancé is fond of feet."

Christy laughed; another emotion to be added to the gamut. "I think he'd be fond of anything that didn't call him out at three in the morning. David is a very organized person—and very determined to keep his life in compartments. He'd hate anything as unpredictable as delivering babies."

"I must admit he has a point," he agreed. "But there are rewards. Bringing a child into the world is a very leveling experience—for a doctor as well as for a woman. Unfortunately, nobody can tell a woman when to go into labor, or how long it will take. Night calls are a part of the deal." He sighed, and then smiled—a smile that made Christy wonder how many women had said yes to him at one time or another. "Perhaps your young man chose for the right reasons, after all. That sort of thing can put a strain on any marriage."

Christy resisted the urge to ask if it had done so for his, and said instead, "I think I'd trust David even if he had to make night calls. He's not the impulsive type. He lives his life according to the rules."

Once more the eyebrows responded. "How long have you known him?"

"Ever since I can remember. We grew up in a small town on Cape Cod, and he was a friend of my two older brothers. It seemed he was always at the house when I was in my teens, almost like another member of the family. Then when he went off to medical school... things just developed naturally. We've been engaged for three years."

"And how much have you seen of him in the past three years? He might have changed."

"You don't know David. He's very single-minded—he had to be, to do as well as he's done."

"Which doesn't answer my question about how much you've seen of him."

The question caused a peculiar tingling as Christy considered how little she had seen of her fiancé. "I've been working in Boston, and he's been in Baltimore interning. Before that, medical school. Even our holidays haven't coincided—David always had to work through holidays, anyway, in order to afford his schooling. We haven't seen a lot of each other in the past three years. I *still* trust him, Dr. Brent, as

I expect him to trust me. Does that answer your question?"

"Either he's exceptionally faithful or you're exceptionally loyal. Or else you're wearing blinkers." His words were cynical but somehow impersonal, and Christy did not take offense. His hand traveled to his forehead and rested there over closed eyes, as though he were pressing away a pain. "Three years is a long time. Too damn long."

"Can I get you something? An aspirin?" asked Christy with a sudden attack of concern. For the past few minutes she had almost forgotten he was an invalid. Belatedly she experienced a pang of remorse for allowing herself to become embroiled in a verbal exchange that must have further sapped his strength.

"No. Pour me a cup of tea. Clear and strong."

With a start she realized she had not thought of the tea once since bringing it. By now it would certainly be strong, and probably bitter, too, for it had been steeping far too long. With a quick apology she perched herself on the very outer edge of the bed to pour it, as far away from him as possible. She handed him the cup and was momentarily disrupted as his fingers brushed hers. Her swift reflex almost spilled the tea as she withdrew her hand abruptly.

"I must go now." Christy stood up, unwilling to risk staying in proximity with a man whose touch seemed to have such a disproportionate effect on her.

Dr. Joshua Brent looked at her with an odd expression. "I won't turn into an animal again, I promise. Please stay for a few more moments. I'm not sleepy now, and I'd like to talk."

"No, really. I must."

"Don't you want to learn about my daughter?" he asked in a dry tone, his eyes becoming speculative on her face. "As I recall, that was your motive in looking over my wife's rooms. If you leave now, I'll have to assume you were lying earlier."

"I wasn't lying," she denied. "I do want to know more."

"Then stay and talk for ten minutes."

"You can tell me about your daughter tomorrow. It *is* very late, and I feel quite...." What was the word that almost came to her lips? *Shaken?* The past twenty minutes or so had disturbed her more than she cared to admit. To be truthful, she felt not at all sleepy. But the physical exhaustion of earlier in the evening had now been replaced by emotional exhaustion. "Quite worn out," she finished.

"You can sleep in tomorrow. It's a long time since I've had a conversation with a woman who doesn't wear a uniform and talk like a Tartar—and even then, the main topic of conversation has been whether to stick the needle in my arm or...elsewhere. Please. I need to talk."

Why had she always had a weakness for people who needed her? Christy hardly knew; but it was that, the admission that he needed some human contact, which kept her from leaving now, despite her own need to escape.

"You can sit on the bed. I won't touch you, I promise. Look—I'll move farther away." He shifted to the center of the bed, beyond touching range. "Or don't you trust me?"

She indicated that she did trust him, and realized, curiously enough, that it was true. All the same her eyes scouted the room to find a chair. Those she saw were heavy upholstered pieces; so eventually, with marked hesitation, she did as he asked, staying precariously close to the edge of the bed.

"It's not catching," he said sardonically, and Christy

knew he was referring to his burns. "Well, now, where were we?"

"About your daughter," Christy reminded him.

"Oh, yes. Natalie's a beautiful little girl. Extraordinary eyes."

"I hear she has your wife's looks."

Something in his face told Christy it had been a mistake to say that, but she decided it was better to confront the matter head-on. She ventured softly, "Are you reluctant to talk about your wife? I'm sure it's still painful for you, but sometimes it helps to say so, and—"

"Natalie looks like my wife, but she's unlike her in every other way," he said in a short voice.

Christy sat quietly, hoping to draw him out by her silence, and at length he started to speak again.

"Why are you so curious about my wife?"

"Because . . . because there are close bonds between a mother and child. I thought it might help me to understand Natalie better. No reason beyond that." But was there a reason beyond that? By now Christy was not even sure of her own motives.

"If you're thinking Natalie's problems might be partly emotional, you're dead wrong. True, she's disturbed now—by her failure to cope. Perhaps fear of failure has something to do with it, too. It's turned her into a quiet child, where she used to be warm and outgoing as a toddler."

"When did you realize Natalie was retarded?" asked Christy, mindful of what Old Tom had said about Mrs. Brent's refusal to recognize the existence of a problem.

He took a moment to formulate his answer. "My wife was a very conscientious mother," he told her finally. "She recognized quite early that Natalie was incapable of many things. It was less obvious to me. But then I didn't keep one eye on the charts—what age Natalie should be buttoning buttons, or using a knife and fork, or tying shoelaces."

"Did your wife discuss it with you?"

"Good Lord, she talked of nothing else!" Dr. Brent's mouth hardened at the corners, and he went on, more revealingly, "But knowing it privately and admitting it publicly are not quite the same. Lana was a beautiful accomplished woman, talented in many ways. Having a retarded child was. . .not in her scheme of things. It was a blow to her pride—a mark of her failure as a mother."

"A lot of parents think that way," said Christy carefully, not wanting to imply any criticism in her words.

"But you're wondering if it was hard on Natalie, aren't you?" he remarked, evidently not fooled by her cautious observation. "Having to live up to expectations, I mean. Well, you can't explain Natalie's problems away with that theory, Miss Sinclair. My wife read all the right books on child care—she studied psychology for a time. Lana believed in being perfect, and she worked very hard at being the perfect mother. In any case Natalie had just as much trouble when she started school."

"What happened then?"

"Nobody else could teach her, either."

"Did the school do any tests—have her assessed in any way?"

"They gave her IQ tests—the usual meaningless stuff. Natalie did badly, of course."

"No—I mean *properly* assessed."

Dr. Brent hesitated visibly. "I'm afraid my wife resisted that sort of thing."

Christy could not conceal all of her surprise, although she managed to keep her unkind thoughts to herself.

But he seemed to sense them. "Does that seem so dreadful? Perhaps it was a mistake—but a very human one, after all. My wife had a reason, you see. For the first time she was beginning to feel that Natalie's problems were not her own fault. She wanted to learn nothing that might force her to believe they were."

"I'm not sure what you mean," said Christy softly, after a moment's silence.

Dr. Brent frowned, and his lean tapered fingers ran a ragged pattern through the ash-blond hair, drawing Christy's eyes. "There's no point in trying to hide the truth from you, Miss Sinclair. When Natalie started school someone suggested to my wife the possibility that her problem was the result of brain damage. That was when Lana decided that I was at fault."

"You?" exclaimed Christy, this time unable to conceal her astonishment. "But—"

"Oh, she had a reason," he said with an impatient scowl. "I delivered Natalie, you see. It wasn't planned that way. Lana had her own obstetrician—doctors make it a rule to avoid treating their own families whenever possible. But one weekend we went to visit friends at their summer camp in the Adirondacks. There was a storm, a road washed out. . .Lana went into labor. You can imagine the rest. She wasn't due for another couple of weeks, or we certainly wouldn't have been in that remote location. And as there wasn't another doctor about. . . ." He halted in his recitation, abruptly.

"Then she blamed you because you delivered Natalie?" probed Christy, hiding her growing unease about the confidences he was imparting.

"Lana believed in natural childbirth, Miss Sinclair," he went on in an arid voice. "But she wasn't built for it. It would have been a difficult birth under the best of circumstances. She was a slender, graceful woman—too slender for childbirth." His eyes traveled openly to Christy's waist, and she felt oddly disturbed at the thought of the comparisons that must be forming in his brain. She shifted on the bed, uncomfortable beneath his gaze, as though it had been his hands, and not his eyes, that measured her. But his voice remained impersonal, and his hands kept to themselves.

"I had a few things with me; a doctor nearly always does. But no forceps. I had to improvise. If I hadn't done so they might both have died, mother and child. At the time Lana objected. I gave her some drug to quiet her—nothing harmful; it's in general use. She was in great distress, you have to understand...nearly hysterical with pain. Later she forgave and forgot, or so I thought. But when the possibility of brain damage came up three years ago, she remembered the circumstances of the birth. She— Oh, God, why am I telling you all this?"

He glowered at Christy, almost resentfully. "You do have a way of getting beneath the surface, don't you? I suppose you've been trained to make people open up. I didn't intend to tell you so much."

Christy sighed. "I haven't been trained for it. I'm a teacher, that's all. Perhaps I stumbled into my line of work because I like listening."

"All the same, I've told you things I thought I'd never tell. Certainly all this has nothing to do with Natalie's problem. Good Lord—my wife may have decided it had some bearing, but I'm equally sure it didn't. I *know* Natalie's difficulties aren't a result of that delivery. Lana fastened on it, that's all, because it was easier for her to blame someone else than admit she had given birth to a less than perfect child. A rather human desire, after all—not wanting to be a failure."

Christy looked at her hands thoughtfully for a few moments. Somehow she guessed that there was more to the story than he had told. But now he seemed to be on guard, and she knew she would learn little more from Dr. Joshua Brent tonight.

As if reading her thoughts, he said dryly, "You're wondering why I didn't insist on getting professional help for Natalie? Well, frankly, I did. Natalie was due to go to a treatment center for the usual battery of tests— she was to have been admitted at the end of January. Naturally, after the fire the whole thing was canceled. It would have been far too upsetting for the child. It seemed best to leave her in boarding school, in familiar surroundings. With her mother dead, and as I've been in hospital for months. . . well, surely you can understand. It's a problem I'll come to grips with in the fall."

"So you're not really sure what's behind Natalie's problems," Christy said, encapsulating what she had learned tonight, "or whether she's even retarded."

"That's right," Dr. Brent agreed, but his voice had become abrupt and dismissive, as though he did not want to discuss the matter anymore. "Pour me another cup of tea before you go, will you?"

Christy obliged and then started toward the door, recognizing his words as a dismissal. But just before she left the room his voice stopped her.

"Don't get the wrong idea, Miss Sinclair." The silver chips of his eyes were distinctly unfriendly. "Natalie's problems weren't caused by any differences between my wife and me. So whatever conclusions you've come to, put them out of that pretty little head of yours."

"I've come to no conclusions," Christy denied, and retreated from the room.

But had she been entirely truthful with him? What did she think about the woman who had been married to this lean disrupting man? Undoubtedly she had been beautiful. Probably a perfect wife and hostess, and perhaps accomplished in a hundred other ways. Had

Joshua Brent been in love with his wife? Her death had left him with a kind of fierce hunger that was frightening.

But what kind of a woman would care more for her own self-image than for the needs of a small child? Dr. Joshua Brent must still be more than half in love with his dead wife if he could not see her for what she evidently had been—a very imperfect perfectionist.

Christy's eyes sought the diamond-and-platinum circle that flashed on her own left hand, as if trying to find strength in it. Why, in view of her own commitment to David, should she find it curiously wrenching to think that Joshua Brent might still care for his wife?

3

CHRISTY SAW NOTHING of her new employer the next day, for while she was in the house his meals were taken to him by one of the local Nantucket women. A veritable squad of cheerful energetic ladies had arrived bright and early to air the house and change the linens, and stock the kitchen with groceries. Cleaning, polishing, scrubbing and shining became the order of the day, and by late afternoon the house gleamed like a new penny. Christy made herself scarce, not wanting to be in the way; and in truth she was relieved that her presence was not required.

Old Tom arranged for one of the local women to stay overnight pending Mrs. Cousins's arrival, and that, too, suited Christy. Already, she realized, circumstances had created an unfortunate intimacy between herself and the man whom everybody seemed to call Dr. Joshua. In the first twelve hours of their acquaintance, following the collision on the ferryboat, she had been angry with him; earned his anger in return; heard details of his life he admitted to telling no one else; seen him in a state of undress that still brought tingles to her skin in remembrance. And she had repulsed his kisses...but perhaps she had not repulsed them as soon as she should have, she decided with scathing honesty. She knew what had happened in the bedroom had not been entirely his fault; that he had been right in claiming to have detected some response. Some response? An understatement, she admitted to herself. Had she pulled away at first contact, she knew that it would have been a brushing of bodies—no more. But she had not pulled away; and the memory of what had happened would remain between them always, no matter how impersonal a relationship she tried to maintain. How could a man she had known for such a short time fill her with such self-doubts? About herself...about David? Last night, after retiring to her own room, she had not slept at all well.

While the women were occupied in cleaning house, Christy took one of the bicycles from the garage and aimed off on twisting country roads. At a low wooden bridge over a creek, she stopped to watch a pair of children catching blue claw crabs with baited fishing lines and long-handled nets. A patch of wild berry bushes occupied some more time, and when Christy returned to Graydunes most of the cobwebs had been swept from her brain. She would not allow herself to become emotionally involved in this summer job, she resolved. It was too draining and tended to interfere with judgment. That night she slept soundly.

But the next day, when Natalie arrived, Christy found all her good resolutions flying out the window. There was something infinitely touching about the reunion: first meeting of father and daughter since the death of the woman they had both loved.

Christy had been down in the rose garden, near the front door, when she heard the first distant sounds of the Jeep returning from the ferryboat. Evidently responding to the sound, Dr. Brent had at once emerged from the front door. He had not gone to meet the ferry himself—possibly because his Mercedes was too small to carry three passengers and luggage; possibly because of the state of his health; but more probably, Christy decided later, because he did not want the emotion-charged meeting to take place in public.

She watched quietly as Dr. Brent walked down the front steps, his eyes fixed intently on the oncoming Jeep and its passengers.

Today, dressed in lean gray flannel slacks and a creamy velour sports shirt open at the neck, he appeared somewhat healthier than he had done on first sight two days before. And—Christy had to admit—more disturbingly virile than ever. He must have spent some time outdoors yesterday, she decided. His compelling ascetic face had a healthier glow about it, and by daylight his hair glinted with a gilded warmth, like beaten silver in the golden day. To Christy he was even more damnably attractive—Oh, *why* must she think that way! She dragged her eyes away from him and back to the Jeep that was braking now at the head of the driveway.

The little girl who must be Natalie tumbled out almost before the vehicle came to a halt, despite the agitated restraining command that came from a stunningly attractive auburn-haired woman seated beside her in the back seat.

"Natalie!" came the sharp order. "Your father's been sick! You mustn't—"

But Natalie was already up the steps and swung high in her father's arms. There were no words between them, but Christy saw the way the little girl snuggled her head into the hard spare shoulders, the way the strong arms came around her, the way the fair head bent down over the child's gleaming dark curls. The reunion was all the more laden with emotion because there were no words spoken. Christy turned her eyes away toward the Jeep, not wanting to witness such a private and poignant scene.

"Natalie!" The woman in the back seat stepped down

from the Jeep, displaying a symphony of lush curves en-
hanced by a clinging pink dress that complemented the
fiery tumble of her hair. She was undeniably beautiful,
but her expression suggested that she felt less than
competent to deal with the young girl who had been put
in her charge. Surely that was not Mrs. Cousins,
thought Christy. The housekeeper had sounded quite
different on the telephone. No, Mrs. Cousins must be
the comfortable-looking, motherly woman still seated
in the front of the Jeep with Old Tom. This must be the
nanny who was scolding away ineffectually, "Natalie,
your father's *burns*—"

"Leave her be," came a deep voice from behind
Christy's shoulder; and then Christy could hear Dr.
Brent retreating into the house with his daughter still
clinging to his shoulders.

"Oh, dear." The auburn-haired woman stared after
her vanishing charge, looking ruffled and annoyed.
"I told her she *mustn't*. I thought she understood;
goodness knows I repeated it often enough. What a
child!"

"Perhaps she forgot when she saw her father. I'm sure
he can look after himself." Christy moved forward,
smiling, and introduced herself.

"I'm Doris Moody," said the other woman, but her
answering smile was distracted. "Please call me Doris.
What a day this has been! That child is a handful. So
difficult to know how to cope with her, and with all the
regular help killed in that fire, there's nobody to give me
pointers."

"I'm sure you'll find she's not so very different from
any other child," Christy reassured her.

"Only slower," frowned Doris Moody.

Christy turned her attention to the other woman,
who must be the housekeeper, now being helped out of

the Jeep. Old Tom, forgetting his arthritis for the moment, was putting on a great show of gallantry.

The housekeeper came bustling forward. "I'm Mrs. Cousins," she said. "You must be Christy Sinclair. You look just like you sound on the telephone—a breath of the country."

Christy laughed and plucked at the fabric of the gaily flowered peasant skirt she had chosen to wear today, with an apple-green blouse. "Children like cheerful colors. I wore it to meet Natalie."

"And she didn't even stay to be introduced," complained Doris Moody, still out of sorts.

"Well, all in good time," allowed Mrs. Cousins in an unruffled voice. Christy had decided earlier during their telephone interview that she was going to like Mrs. Cousins, and now she reaffirmed the decision in her mind. The housekeeper was a pleasantly rounded woman in her late middle years, with curly short-cropped gray hair and an unpretentious face. She was one of those women who manage to exude an aura of efficiency and femininity all at once. Looking at her, Christy could not help but think of cherry cobblers hot from the oven and cheerful visits in polished-copper kitchens.

As for Doris Moody—well, it was too soon to decide, thought Christy as she helped the new arrivals into the house with their luggage. The woman had been hired through an employment agency, she knew that; and doubtless it had been difficult enough for Mrs. Cousins to find anyone suitable on such short notice. And it shouldn't matter whether she liked the woman or not, Christy pondered, since their duties would not overlap. Doris Moody would have charge of the child during rising times and mealtimes and nap times and bedtimes, but she would exert no authority during the hours when Christy was teaching.

The lessons were to start Monday. Nine until noon, it had been decided; then, after lunch and a short rest, the work would resume at two and continue until four-thirty. A total of five and a half hours of instruction was more than enough for a child whose attention span, Christy had been warned, was minimal. But on the other hand it seemed little enough to do for the money she was being paid—and it was with this in mind that she sought, a short time later, to offer a helping hand to Mrs. Cousins. Already, with the housekeeper ensconced in the house for no more than an hour, friendly smells of baked ham and freshly percolated coffee permeated the sunny kitchen.

"Couldn't I do something?" volunteered Christy as she entered the room. "Natalie's still up with her father, and Doris Moody's with them, too, for all I know. I feel quite useless at the moment."

"You'll have your work cut out for you soon enough," observed Mrs. Cousins cheerfully. "You haven't seen a grater around here, have you? Mercy me—the worst of any kitchen is getting to find out where things are kept. I do wish that local lady hadn't left."

Christy had used the grater in the making of the cheese omelet, and she located it without difficulty. "Can I do it for you?"

"Why, thank you. Not too much of the peel, mind—just enough for flavor. Gives a real lift to a lemon meringue pie. Miss Natalie says it's her father's favorite."

Christy set to work with the grater, remarking, "There's nothing wrong with Natalie's memory, then."

"Land sakes, no, if you can get the child to talk at all. All inside herself, she is, and no wonder, poor wee thing. Losing her mother and all—although the school says she's mostly over that now. All the same, I had to speak to her half a dozen times before she would answer. Just looks at you, eyes like pansies, and so pretty it's hard to think she's a mite slow in the head. Never could tell me the name of her own favorite food. When I asked, she just held up her fingers like this—" a floury hand went up in the air, demonstrating "—and she wouldn't say anything, even though I asked her several times. I don't think she understood me at all, poor lamb! It wasn't until I turned to asking her about her dad's favorites that she opened her mouth. And even then it took her a while to answer."

"Perhaps she has a hearing problem." Christy finished with the grater and went to rinse it at the sink.

"Oh, she heard me; I knew by her eyes! No, she's not too quick, that little one, and come Monday you'll have all you can do to try and teach her her letters. Such a shame, her age and not past kindergarten. All the same, she seems warm and friendly enough, if a little quiet. And every once in a while she speaks right up—just when you're not expecting it."

"Oh?" prompted Christy, pouring herself a cup of coffee from the steaming percolator on the stove and pulling a chair up to the scrubbed wooden table where Mrs. Cousins was rolling out pastry.

"Well, yes, and I don't think that nanny liked too well what she said." Mrs. Cousins glanced upward, and Christy thought she detected the beginnings of a twinkle in the woman's warm eyes. "I'll tell you, it was a good thing we were about to get off the ferryboat, or there might have been the merry devil to pay!"

"Oh? What did Natalie say?"

"'You look like your name.' Imagine that! Came right out with it, staring with those great big eyes, all calm and solemn like saucers. Well, I'll tell you, that Doris Moody, she's been a bit flustered ever since. Of course I

just swept the wee tyke away and told her her father
wouldn't want her saying things like that." Mrs.
Cousins put down the rolling pin, and the chuckle
that had been threatening at last found voice. "Yes,
for all that it was the wrong thing to say, it certainly
seemed like the truth. You should have seen that
woman's face!"

Christy laughed despite herself. "No wonder she
seemed upset when you arrived. I expect she was still off
balance. All the same, it's too bad Natalie made the
remark."

"I expect it's hard to teach her not to say things out of
turn," remarked Mrs. Cousins. "What did you make of
the child?"

"I haven't met her yet."

"And the doctor? Dr. Joshua, he told me to call him. I
met him at the nursing home, of course, for I went there
to be hired. And I talked to him on the phone after that,
a dozen times. My, it was a shock when he phoned yesterday to say he was here! I never would have thought
the man could drag himself from bed so soon. But he's
looking a sight better already. He must have the con-
stitution of a horse! From what the nurses told me, he's
been through purgatory and back. A bit strained and
grim about the mouth, it's true, but it's only to be expected, under the circumstances. Well, it's a shame, for
he seems like a fine upstanding man. And I hear his pa-
tients think the world of him. Was he at the house when
you arrived?"

"Yes," answered Christy, remembering only too well
the embarrassing circumstances that had led her to his
bedroom.

Mrs. Cousins patted the pastry into place and skillfully fluted the edge as she rotated the pie plate. "Well, I
daresay a little fattening up will do him good. He's too

thin by half, and such a tall man, too! That hospital food just isn't—"

But whatever uncomplimentary thing she had been about to say about hospital food remained unsaid, for at that moment Doris Moody sauntered into the kitchen. Her mouth had lost its petulant expression and now wore a small secretive smile, almost a triumphant look. With the smile, and with her hair teased to a bouffant halo, she seemed totally self-possessed now. She moved with the languor of a cat—a woman sure of her own seductive powers, and probably for good reason, Christy reflected wryly.

"Dr. Joshua would like a cup of coffee," Doris said to Mrs. Cousins pointedly, without making any move to get it herself. She threw herself down on a kitchen chair and stretched her arms lazily, drawing attention to voluptuous breasts. "Make that two, will you? Both black. And some juice for Natalie."

Mrs. Cousins's lips thinned, but she started to wipe the flour from her hands.

"I'll get it," offered Christy swiftly, and moved to the cupboard for mugs. With her back turned to the kitchen table she was able to school her expression and conceal the flare of annoyance she had felt at Doris Moody's presumptuous manner.

"I do believe I'm going to like this godforsaken island after all." The voice behind Christy's back was a silken purr. "Come to think of it, put the whole pot on the tray, will you? Dr. Joshua says he has coffee starvation, and so have I. By the way, Mrs. Cousins, he says he'll take his supper upstairs with Natalie in her room. You'll have to put a tray together later. What time shall I tell him to expect it?"

"Six-thirty," came Mrs. Cousins's abrupt reply, betraying a shortness that had not been apparent in her earlier conversation with Christy.

"Call me when it's ready. I'll take it up to him."

"Perhaps it would be best if I set a proper table for the doctor," suggested Mrs. Cousins. "Surely there's a suitable one in Natalie's room."

"I'll do it," said Doris. "He wouldn't want just anybody traipsing through the child's quarters."

"Are you sure it isn't too much trouble for you?" returned Mrs. Cousins in a dry tone.

Doris Moody seemed to miss the sarcasm and answered airily, "No trouble at all. I have nothing else to do at the moment, except watch that that child doesn't make too much bother of herself."

"Perhaps Dr. Brent wants to be bothered." Christy, who had been listening with growing antagonism, vented some of her annoyance by jerking the punch opener into a can of chilled juice. She poured a glass. "He hasn't seen Natalie since the accident—not since Mrs. Brent's death."

"Oh?" Doris Moody tilted a brow upward in mild interest as Christy placed a completed tray in front of her. "Well, I suppose that's why she's making such a nuisance of herself. That child won't listen to a word I say! But I expect I'll set that to rights in a day or two."

"You'd better, hadn't you?" returned Christy with a smile that was a shade too nice. "Else there's not much point in your working here at all—is there, Miss Moody?"

Doris Moody looked at her suspiciously, with darkening eyes. Mrs. Cousins, sensing the beginning of a battle, broke in quickly, "Oh, Doris...will you be eating upstairs in the nursery, too, with Natalie?"

"Why, I...." Doris Moody's face fell a little, and the flustered look that had been apparent on her arrival now returned, destroying some of her looks. Then her mouth firmed up again, and she finished, with her eyes on Christy, "I suppose I will, as I'm in charge of the child at mealtimes. And that's the whole point of my working here—*isn't* it?" She picked up the tray and stalked to the door. But before she left she turned back and added, putting Christy firmly in her place, "And it's *Mrs.* Moody, Miss, er, Sinclair. I'm a widow. I lost my husband only a few months ago. I have that in common with the doctor. Perhaps that's why he asked *me* to call him Joshua."

Mrs. Cousins stood with her hands on her hips, staring after the woman's receding figure. "Well, I never!" she said at last, when it was safe to do so. "That woman is a caution. I can't think why I hired her!"

Christy laughed, with a great deal more casualness than she felt. "Oh, I suppose I shouldn't have baited her." Then her eyes twinkled at Mrs. Cousins, releasing those little glints of gold. "But why *did* you hire her?"

Mrs. Cousins sighed. "There wasn't too much to choose from, I'm afraid, for I wanted a good swimmer to mind Natalie. And she has that qualification if nothing else. She used to teach ornamental swimming before she married. And I suppose I was taken in by that sob story about being a widow, and finding it hard to get work because she had very little training and no recent references. Widow indeed! Her husband committed suicide. Now I wonder if I don't know why."

"Well, I suppose she's to be pitied for that," Christy sighed. "But she is rather abrasive. I can't say I'll miss her at suppertime. With luck maybe she'll take all her meals upstairs."

"Given half a chance, she will," grumped Mrs. Cousins, popping her pie shells in the oven. "But not unless the good doctor does, too. That woman may be a slouch about some things, but not when it comes to spotting a lonely man! She's wearing an Available sign a mile high, and don't think I didn't see it on the ferry-boat this afternoon. Making eyes at every man old enough to have hair on his chest, and a few that weren't."

"I'm surprised she took a job looking after a child," Christy remarked.

"Husband-hunting, I imagine. Her interest perked when she heard Dr. Joshua was a widower and a big New York practitioner. And you can be sure she's made good note of the fact that she and he have a wing of the house to themselves—but for the child, of course."

Christy felt her stomach do a sick little flop. Now why should she care about that? And yet it had been an instinctive reaction, for the thought had not occurred to her before. She busied her hands with stirring her coffee and tried to govern her unruly thoughts. But unwanted visions of a gaunt blond man with a sensual mouth kept returning to her—a burning mouth, bending hungrily over a willing widow's lips. David, David, David, she said to herself fiercely; but her fiancé's face remained elusive, refusing to recreate itself in her imagination.

"I don't fancy she's Dr. Joshua's type," Mrs. Cousins went on, noting nothing amiss, for she still had her back turned. "All the same, you never know. It's hard for a man to refuse what's offered, especially a widowed man, for he'll be extra susceptible right now. And you can be sure she'll be offering! Why would Dr. Joshua turn her down? Unless the man's a saint."

Why indeed? And Dr. Joshua was not a saint. Remembering the naked need she had seen in that lean hungry face not forty-eight hours earlier, Christy knew it would be only a matter of time until Doris Moody found her way into Joshua Brent's arms. The thought made her feel actively nauseated, and she gave up trying to think of David at all.

4

SUNDAY MORNING CAME and with it, at last, an introduction to young Natalie Brent. Christy, clad in denims and a bright plaid shirt, was already eating when Doris Moody brought the child down to breakfast. Today Doris wore tight scarlet pants and a white silk shirt that left very little to the imagination. Once more, she had a distraught look about her.

Natalie's face was pink, and her eyes wore a sheen that told of recent tears. The little girl at once ran over to Mrs. Cousins and found herself folded instantaneously into comforting arms.

"Well, there, Miss Natalie, why so sad this morning? What's the matter, lamb?" Mrs. Cousins asked in a warm voice.

Doris Moody, evidently out of sorts, dropped onto a chair at the kitchen table. "I expect she wants her father, that's all. He said he wasn't to be bothered this morning. Well, I don't know how he could help but be bothered, with all that crying and caterwauling! I've never seen such a fuss about putting on a pair of shoes."

"Perhaps she's not ready to do it yet." Christy kept her voice pleasant, mindful of Natalie's presence. "Laces can seem very complicated for small fingers. I hear Natalie's still learning to manage them."

"Well, I know *that*." Doris Moody stared at Christy resentfully. "But she doesn't even seem to have the sense to let me do it for her. No brains at all."

Christy's jaw dropped, but before she could say anything, Mrs. Cousins said the words for her. "How dare you say such a thing! Perhaps you'd best put your own brains to some use, Mrs. Doris Moody! I was given authority to hire you, and I expect I can fire you, too, as Dr. Joshua is still half an invalid and he's left the running of the house up to me."

The other woman appeared to be seriously taken aback for a moment. But then she composed herself, and slowly a small knowing smile came to her lips. "Can you?" she said softly. Her eyes glittered. "I don't think so. Not after . . . after last night."

Her meaning was clear to everyone in the room—everyone, that is, but the child whose head was still buried in Mrs. Cousins's ample lap.

But now Natalie's head came up, and she stared at Doris Moody with large damp purple-pansy eyes. Although she said nothing, the stare seemed to make the woman uncomfortable. Doris added, almost nervously, as if in explanation to the child, "Now, you went to sleep last night, Natalie. That's all I meant, darling. You were a good little girl for your nanny."

"For my dad," corrected an unsmiling Natalie.

"For your daddy, too," agreed Doris Moody in a soothing voice, but it was accompanied by a little gleam of triumph in the general direction of Christy and Mrs. Cousins. "Daddy was *very* pleased with you, darling, for sleeping so nicely."

Christy, sickened, pushed the remains of her breakfast aside. "Do you like blueberry pancakes, Natalie?" she said brightly in an effort to change the subject.

"I'll make them," offered Mrs. Cousins, but Natalie clung to her apron, not wanting to let her go. The little girl turned her tearstained eyes to Christy.

"Who are you?"

"I'm Christy.

"Christy who?"

"Christy Sinclair. You can call me Christy; everybody does. It's short for Christine."

Doris Moody interjected maliciously, "Miss Sinclair is your teacher, darling. Do you understand what that means? Teacher. She's going to teach you the alphabet. You know, T-E-A-C-H—"

"No!" exploded Natalie ferociously, and the head went back into the lap. "I don't want a teacher."

"I'm not a teacher today; it's Sunday," Christy said with a cheerfulness that was about one millimeter deep. "Today I'm your blueberry-pancake maker. Would you like some, with syrup and sausages?"

"No," came the muffled reply from Mrs. Cousins's skirt.

"I'll take two." Doris Moody settled back in her chair and pulled out a pack of cigarettes. Her eyes fanned toward Christy and stayed there, challenging. "No sausages, but I'll have a cup of coffee while I'm waiting."

Christy felt a slow burn begin. Oh, if only Natalie were not here! But the child was here—so she replied, levelly enough, "The frying pan's right over there, Doris. And the batter, too. Perhaps Natalie would eat some if you made them for her."

"No," came a small voice.

"Well, now," Mrs. Cousins coaxed at the small dark head in her lap. "What *do* you like eating for breakfast, Natalie? You must have something or you'll fade away."

"Oh, *that* one," said Doris Moody impatiently. "She doesn't like anything that needs a knife and fork. Poked around at that baked ham last night and hardly ate a thing. Always wanting to use her fingers."

Christy and Mrs. Cousins looked at each other with dawning comprehension and then broke into delighted grins over Natalie's head.

"I don't see anything to smile about," Doris complained waspishly. She got to her feet and went to the stove to pour herself some coffee, evidently giving in to the realization that nobody intended to do it for her. "Perhaps I'll just have a sausage or two, as they're already cooked." She helped herself to several and returned to the table.

"I'll bet you like toast, Natalie," suggested Christy. Without waiting for an answer, she went over to the counter and dropped two slices of brown bread into the pop-up toaster.

"And hot dogs," said Mrs. Cousins with a twinkle. "And hamburgers."

"And carrot sticks," Christy went on, making a game of it; for she had seen Natalie's small beautifully shaped head come up, and the beginnings of interest in the violet eyes.

"And celery," laughed Mrs. Cousins.

"And crackers and cheese."

"And apples."

"And bananas."

"What are you two talking about?" came a petulant interjection.

"And sandwiches," returned Mrs. Cousins, ignoring Doris Moody.

"And sausages." Christy put two of them on a plate and buttered the toast to go alongside. "Have you ever eaten sausages with your fingers, Natalie? I often do. It's all right, if your fingers are clean."

"Of course they're clean." Doris glared balefully at Christy. "But she has to learn to use a knife and fork. You know that."

"Of course," agreed Christy promptly. "And I'm sure Natalie knows it, too. But not every meal. We'll stick to finger foods this morning."

"Are you questioning my authority?" bristled Doris Moody. "Dr. Joshua—"

"You're quite right," Christy broke in quickly, trying to avert an unpleasant scene. "You *are* in charge at mealtimes, of course. If you prefer Natalie to eat with a knife and fork, by all means change her menu. As I said, there's the batter, and the pan's still hot."

Doris didn't answer, but her lips thinned unpleasantly, and Christy knew her own interference would not soon be forgotten.

"Lands sakes, Natalie," Mrs. Cousins observed, at last relinquishing the child from her lap, "you must be starving after last night's supper. Baked ham and scalloped potatoes, and cheese sauce on the broccoli. And then lemon pie for dessert—I'm sure you hardly ate a bite! If I'd had more sense, I'd have understood long ago. Now eat up, there's a good girl."

But there was no need to urge Natalie further, for she had set to work with ten fingers and a will, and before long the toast and sausages, along with a sectioned orange and two glasses of milk, had been completely demolished.

"Now why didn't I see that sooner?" said Mrs. Cousins some minutes later, wagging her gray head pleasurably. She and Christy were alone now, for nanny and child had at last left, with the stated intention of going down to the beach. "All the time, those fingers in the air meant something! Well, it's me that's a little slow, and that's a fact."

"How could you know?" Christy answered as they cleared the table together. "It would help if Natalie spoke up once in a while. She's a very quiet child. She needs to open up a bit."

"And I don't think she'll open up for that—that—" Mrs. Cousins made a face "—that *bitch*. I don't like to use the word, but there isn't another one that says it."

"You couldn't have put it better," agreed Christy with a chuckle, but then she became serious. "Why don't you speak to the doctor? About replacing Doris Moody, I mean. I'm sure her company can't be doing Natalie any good."

"Well, now...." Mrs. Cousins stopped to reflect. "I don't like to upset him when he's feeling poorly. And in spite of what I said, I *can't* fire the woman. The employment agency insisted on a contract, with Dr. Joshua's name on it. Besides, I fancy he's not the man to fire someone without a fair trial. And I'm sure when he's around she's all sugar and spice."

"And everything nice," concurred Christy dryly, remembering only too well that Dr. Joshua had been quite ready to fire *her* on a moment's notice. "But a week from now it may be even harder. He may become dependent on her in...in other ways."

"You don't believe that about last night, do you?" Mrs. Cousins shot Christy a curious glance. "Not that it wouldn't happen in time, mind! I said so myself. But not so soon. And not with Natalie sleeping in the next room. That woman was lying."

"I wonder," murmured Christy, wishing the intrusive images would stop dragging at her mind. As they did for the rest of the day....

THERE WERE NO LESSONS planned for the day, just as Christy had indicated to Natalie. Unneeded, she found she had too much time to think. She took a short swim in the morning; then, in an effort to drive away the demons that drummed in her head, and not wanting to confront Doris Moody at another mealtime, she packed herself a picnic lunch and set off about one o'clock toward the island's interior, choosing the loneliest back roads she could find. This time she pedaled with a fine fury, until her pained muscles cried out for relief.

Next thing I'll be taking cold showers, Christy scolded herself angrily. In venting her frustrations, she hardly noticed the restful rolling windswept moors and the ruffled waters stretching far into Nantucket Sound. A marsh hawk swooped down in chase of some unseen prey. A brace of pheasant and several wild ducks rose, crying, from reedy little ponds nestled between hummocks of long grass. A jackrabbit loped nervously away, long ears streaming, at Christy's approach. She noticed none of it.

Why had she never felt perturbed in this way about David—even knowing that he occasionally found himself a date when attending mixed parties in Baltimore? He had been quite open about this fact, claiming that a female partner was required for some social occasions; and Christy had known that was true enough. Visions of David with other women had never troubled her. Perhaps because he was so stubbornly methodical, so self-disciplined, so predictable, so...good heavens, not *boring!* How could she ever think of attaching such a word to David? David had too much drive and ambition to be thought of as boring. And yet she knew she had indeed done so.

But then, David had never kissed her with the kind of ferocity and hunger she could still almost taste on her lips, three days after the fact.

David. His caresses had been pleasurable enough and on one remembered occasion had become passionate and demanding. That time he had whispered a suggestion into Christy's ear before things had gone very far.

"No, I won't," she had said, drawing back.

"Everybody else is on the pill," he had pointed out, at once in control of himself. David was like that—he had a strong grip on his emotions. "I'm not ready to get married yet, Christy, and I can't afford to have all my plans turned upside down for a moment of madness."

"And I refuse to *plan* for a moment of madness," she had said, angered briefly by the methodical way he approached everything, even lovemaking.

From there the matter had gone into stalemate, and David's kisses had remained perfunctory. *He* had no intention of producing an unwanted child. And she—was it because she was unsure of David, or was it because of the old-fashioned notions instilled in her by her family?

David had always been so controlled. Perhaps that was why visions of Joshua Brent kept burning in her brain. He had not been controlled—and neither, for a few moments, had she. And she thought she knew why: frustration. Sheer, old-fashioned, ornery frustration. Christy was twenty-four years old and altogether ready for the thing that seemed to be an accepted fact of life nowadays. Why had she never wanted to give in to David's demands?

Oh, damn Dr. Joshua Brent, and damn the pill, and most of all damn David! She struck at the pedals ferociously with her sneakered feet and wet tears of frustration stung at her eyelids when the bicycle chain came free of its sprockets, clattering noisily against the spokes of the wheel.

"Oh, *no!*"

Now she would have to walk back, for she had no tools with which to repair the damage. Five or six miles at the very least, unless some chance motorist happened by and took pity on her. And cars were few and far between on this rutted back road, especially on a Sunday and before the start of the real summer season. Dolefully she sat down to eat a belated lunch and gather strength for the return trip.

David: she would phone him tonight, and that would put things back into perspective. This afternoon would be even better, but she knew she could not phone him, not before midnight, for his duties as an intern kept him busy until then. All the same, the decision gave her some comfort, and it was with a certain tranquillity, on the surface at least, that she finished her lunch and started trudging homeward, pushing the now useless bicycle.

Deep in her own thoughts, Christy had not noticed that the sky, which had been streaky that morning, had with the advancing afternoon become leaden. The first fat drops of water startled her, and she glanced upward to see that the lowering sky was swollen with rain. A cloudburst seemed imminent. She hurried along the road, but progress was slow with the bicycle in tow. At last she spotted an old lean-to—perhaps an ancient sheep-shearing shed, left from days when the animals used to graze the island. She pushed the bicycle through the ditch and across the lumpy moors, and took refuge.

And not a moment too soon. The heavens opened, and rain lashed at the abandoned hut as if its only goal were to drive the sagging roof right into the ground. But the ancient hand-hewn timbers held, and the rotted shingles above them; and in this leaky shelter shared only with a few shivering field mice, Christy remained relatively dry and comfortable. However, it was a long time before the rain eased enough that she could consider the trip back to Graydunes. How much time had passed? An hour...two? Christy hardly knew. She had removed her wristwatch earlier for the swim and had forgotten it in her haste to be out of the house. Surely it must be approaching the dinner hour by now. Mrs.

Cousins might be worried...but there was no help for it. The house must be at least four miles away even now, and the distance had to be walked.

Truthfully, Christy was not even sure of exactly how far she had traveled earlier today, in her spurt of furious pedaling. Could it be that she had covered more territory than she thought? Well, at least there was no need to push the bicycle all the way home: Old Tom could come for it tomorrow in the Jeep. She pushed it under a growth of bracken at the side of the lean-to and set off on foot, unencumbered.

But the roads were sodden and the going hard. Christy plodded along disconsolately, her way made no easier by the caking of mud that clung to her shoes and the cuffs of her blue jeans. One mile, two...but by the time she had walked an estimated three miles, it seemed she was hardly closer to her goal than before. How far *had* she gone earlier? At least she had no doubts about being on the right road. From the occasional vantage point on a rise of land, she could see the coastline spread before her, and the darkening waters of the Sound.

The darkening waters. Yes it *was* getting dark, Christy realized. Perhaps the sun had already set behind that heavy overcast. If so, it must be at least two hours later than she would have guessed in her wildest imaginings. Setting her chin into a determined line, she increased her pace, refusing to give in to leg muscles that were now in a state of total excruciating rebellion.

Darkness descended relentlessly.

The sounds and lights of an approaching automobile offered no more than a moment's comfort, for the car was heading in the wrong direction. To accept a ride, assuming one was offered, would only take her many miles away from Graydunes. As the car neared, Christy averted her eyes from the stabbing headlights, stayed on the far side of the road and hurried onward.

The car screeched to a halt, and only then did she take time to pick out the dim outline of a vehicle that was low-slung and sleek and unmistakable.

"What the *hell* are you up to?" said an exasperated voice out of the lowered window. Then a door swung open, automatically switching on the interior light. The little pool of luminescence on pale ash-blond hair confirmed Christy's guess.

"Oh...Dr. Brent," she said rather stupidly, half in relief and half in alarm at the leaping of pulses over which she seemed to have no control.

"Get in," he said grimly. "Don't you know you've turned the whole house topsy-turvy? This is a hell of a time to be out walking."

Christy opened the passenger door and got in with a rueful glance at her muddied feet. "I wasn't walking," she denied. "I was out bike riding."

"Without a bike?" he returned sarcastically, tilting a brow upward. Then the car door closed, swallowing both of them in darkness but for the faint glow from the dashboard lights. For an instant, before Joshua started the car again, it seemed as though the darkness and loneliness of the road bound them together in a forced intimacy—an intimacy Christy felt she could not break by answering his question.

But then he started to drive, maneuvering the car in a three-point turn, and Christy found her missing voice. "The bike broke down. I left it in a safe place a few miles along the road. I'm sorry if I've caused trouble."

"You have a way of attracting it," came the dry reply as he accelerated. "Ever since you bumped into me on the ferryboat you seem to have done very little else. Old

Tom Maybee has been out hunting for you for two hours now in the Jeep."

"I'm sorry," she repeated helplessly. "And I'm sorry you had to come out, too. I didn't realize how far I had gone, and then the rain—I do apologize. I suppose you've all been worrying, too."

His voice cut through her apologies. "Don't flatter yourself, Miss Sinclair. I wouldn't have noted your absence at all if I hadn't sent for you after Natalie's bedtime."

"Sent for me?" Her heart did a quick leap—and plummeted at his next words.

"I expect my household to run smoothly, Miss Sinclair. Heaven knows I pay enough for the privilege. With three women supposedly good at their jobs, I can't see how it can be in an uproar already. Don't you know your duties don't start until tomorrow?"

"Why, yes," she answered with a sinking feeling.

"Then why are you interfering at Natalie's mealtimes?"

"Has Doris Moody been complaining about me?"

"Frankly, yes."

"I . . . I don't think she should have gone to you about it. It was a small matter, really, and solved without conflict."

"That's not what I heard."

"Then she can't have told you the whole truth. Don't you want to hear my side of it? We didn't fight at all. Why, I wouldn't want to do that in front of Natalie. The whole thing passed right over her head, I'm sure, and—"

"Oh?" he broke in, his voice grim. "Don't be so certain. When Doris brought the matter up, Natalie was there. It was my daughter's remark that made me decide Doris's version must be the truth."

"Remark?" queried Christy. "What did Natalie say?"

"Only two words: 'Christy won.' Christy *won*. You couldn't have won if you hadn't been fighting. For God's sake, how could you think the child wouldn't notice? Natalie may be slightly retarded, Miss Sinclair, but she's not totally without perception. You can deny that you fought—but can you deny that you *won*?"

Christy turned numb at the vehemence in his tone. "No, I can't deny that," she said in a low and level voice.

"In that case it seems there's no more to say. I'm willing to forget this incident as long as it doesn't happen again. Just because I've been ill doesn't mean I'll submit to having my life, or Natalie's, disrupted by a bunch of squabbling hens. Perhaps I've been too used to a wife who made sure the household ran like a well-oiled machine— Oh, Lord!" In the darkness Christy could sense, rather than see, the way one hand left the steering wheel and ran a ragged pattern through his hair. Then control returned to his voice, and his hand to its task.

"Your responsibility is lesson time, no more. I won't have any fighting, especially when it has to do with Natalie. Doris may not be perfect—who is? But she's only trying to do her job, and it's not an easy one. Don't poach on her preserves!"

How could he be so unfair? Christy compressed her lips over the desire to fling accusations back in his face and stifled an equally childish impulse to cry out denials. To do so would put her on the same petty level as Doris Moody, and might only seem to give credence to whatever had been said about her. No; the matter was best dropped. This morning's altercation would soon be forgotten, especially if she made sure to stay out of the other woman's way. And in time, Christy was becoming sure, Doris Moody would tie her own noose and put her head in it. It was only to be hoped she did not hurt Natalie too much in the process.

The headlights picked out the white stones that spelled Graydunes, and the car crunched onto the gravel of the circular driveway. Joshua guided it skillfully through the open door of the garage and into its parking space. He turned off the headlights before he spoke again, and darkness was Christy's only barrier against his next cold words.

"If I hear of anything unpleasant happening again, Miss Sinclair, I won't hesitate to fire the person responsible. My daughter's welfare means a great deal to me. Don't expect me to show you any quarter just because I happened to... to kiss you the other day, in a moment of weakness. That didn't mean a thing. Not a damn thing—except that you happened to be there."

"And I'm sorry I was!" Christy turned her back to him and fumbled with the door handle. Haste and darkness made her fingers clumsy, but she managed to open the door, causing the car's interior light to switch on automatically. She swiveled her feet outward, ready to race for safety, but in the next moment her shoulders were seized with compelling force. "Don't run away when I'm speaking to you!" Joshua snapped.

He yanked her back, and she tumbled hard against him, her head falling back to expose the long smooth curve of her throat. She lay there with heart beating hard, her eyes flashing defiance, her chest heaving. With the low gearshift digging at her spine it was a difficult and uncomfortable position, and she had little leverage to push herself upright. One arm was against Joshua's lap, totally trapped by his gaunt body, while the other was nearly as effectively confined by the padded steering wheel.

The light from the roof light above his head glanced

across his pale hair, sheening it, while his face remained in shadow. The silvered blondness, so in contrast to the grim darkness of his expression, sent frissons of warning chasing along her veins. Christy knew the situation was fraught with peril. If Doris had been telling the truth, Joshua might no longer be in a state of frustration, but that didn't alter the dangerous sexual magnetism he exuded. She saw the harsh set of his jaw, the tightened muscles in his throat, but it was not his anger she feared. It was simply *him*.

She managed to wriggle her left arm free of the wheel, only to find her entire torso pinned and held in the circle of one powerful arm.

His eyes blazed with silver fire. "Do you understand what I'm saying?" The words hissed out through furiously clenched teeth. "I care a great deal about my daughter. Along with all her other problems she happens to be in a difficult emotional state right now. I won't have you upsetting her again!"

Christy was too proud to defend herself properly but too angry to keep her silence altogether. "I imagine she's a lot more upset by that—that merry Moody widow and whatever bedroom waltzes the two of you were up to last night! You're not very fastidious about sex, are you? You're so damn impatient to make love you don't give a hoot who's on the receiving end. Anyone who happens along will do!"

Joshua sucked in his breath and glared at her, some dark emotion growing in his expression.

For reasons Christy didn't stop to analyze the storm clouds in his eyes filled her with a wild sense of exhilaration and power. She forgot to think of the impending danger. Unwittingly driven, she continued her taunts. "If you weren't wearing sexual blinkers about that woman, you'd see she—"

He pulled her close and stopped her mouth with a kiss. It started in anger, a seal to stop the provocation of her words, but that didn't stop the strong wave of desire that washed through Christy in the moment when his mouth connected with hers. As his lips took hers, she reacted to the taste of him with a shock of pure unadulterated pleasure. Heat swept over the surface of her skin. When his encircling arm yanked her close against him, her body arched of its own accord. For one unthinking moment she met his plundering lips eagerly, surrendering herself to the impassioned kiss.

Almost immediately Joshua's anger ceded to other, even more primitive instincts. As their mouths clung, the mold of his lips softened. He groaned low in his throat, and then she felt his fingers moving hurriedly on the buttons of the cotton shirt she wore, felt the coolness of night air strike her breasts as he loosed her brassiere, felt the urgency and tremble of his hand as he brushed the coverings aside.

Her moment of madness didn't last. Beneath the arm trapped in Joshua's lap she became aware of the ready springing response of his body. The instant and potent burgeoning of desire reminded her that he was a man with too many surges of sudden passion and too few qualms about using any passing woman. She fought her lips free, and her eyes came open to see his silvery head descending toward her throat, half impelled by her own hand. Oh, God. What insane impulse had led her to twine her fingers into his hair?

He was moving his opened mouth across her collarbone and the small delicate hollow between—way station on a trail that would soon lead his kisses to her breasts. Christy searched for strength, thinking of David, thinking of the ring on her left hand. She could see it, the platinum gleam half lost against the paleness of Joshua's hair. . . .

She forced her fingers to relax their grip at his scalp, but his demanding lips had already earned surrender from the tiny fluttering pulse at the sensitive base of her throat. And now it was not only Joshua she had to fight but the delirium of sensation he had provoked.

The ring was reminder enough she must not give in, but Christy was too well pinioned to fight free. Sandwiched into place and held against the steering wheel, effectively trapped by the uncomfortable confinement of space, she was virtually a captive of his passion. One arm was still totally imprisoned against his lap, so only one of her hands was able to move—a small defense indeed, considering his superior strength. Moreover, remembering his scars this time, she didn't wish to use a fist to fight him, although she would if she had to. Even her feet were useless as weapons, for her jeans-clad legs still dangled out the open passenger door, where they had been emerging at the moment he'd flung her across his lap.

She could think of no easy way to extricate herself, and yet she had to. He had not yet kissed her naked breasts, but the mere feel of his fevered breath, now swiftly approaching the goal, had brought her nipples budding into life.

"Stop," she begged, aghast at her body's betrayal.

That brought his head briefly upward. She saw his eyes laden with obsessive desire, his mouth heavy with sensuousness, a muscle in his temple twitching, its visible tempo warning her of his smoldering need for conquest. His hungry eyes raked her bared breasts, fastening on the traitorous evidence of desire. She was overwhelmingly conscious of her vulnerable exposure—the milky curves undarkened by sun, the softness and the hardness of them laid open to his inspection beneath the roof light of the car. The taut nipples, dark against the paleness, betrayed a state of high arousal she would never have admitted to in words.

She used her free hand in an attempt to restore some degree of modesty. The ineffectual move merely caused a pained darkening of his eyes. "Oh, God," he muttered thickly, "are you trying to drive me out of my mind? You tell me no, but your body tells me yes, arching and quivering one moment and pulling back the next. You're too old to play virginal games like that."

"Stop," she begged again, but he merely manacled her wrist and slowly pulled it aside with the left hand that encircled her.

"Let's see what your body says," he breathed huskily.

"Arrogant bastard!" Christy cried, feeling near desperation. Panting, with her chest heaving, she fought to find some shred of willpower. And then he began to assault her with a new weapon—the weapon of seductive gentleness.

His right hand was free. With his blazing eyes riveted on her bodily responses, he used one finger to drag a slow tantalizing circle around a nipple, as if mapping a claim, delineating its outer boundaries. He brushed its very peak, forcing his fingertips to be utterly gentle. The crest trembled beneath his touch. "Admit it—as your body does," he muttered, his voice guttural with need. "How can you pretend you don't want this when I can see for myself you do?"

Christy had closed her eyes. She was moaning and stirring softly beneath the featherlight stimulation. She whispered, "No, no. . . ."

But her body belied her words. Feeling her shuddering submission, Joshua bent his head. He dropped a trail of ardent kisses where his fingertips had been tantalizing her breast.

As his lips fastened closely and his flickering tongue began to stab at the hardened nipple, her eyes sprang open. She thought she could not bear the erotic thrill that coursed through her, causing her to arch unthinkingly even while her mind told her to stop. "Please let me go," she pleaded faintly.

An anguish of contradictory feeling was fermenting inside her. Her brain warned her not to respond, but her flesh was being forced into mindless singing response by the beautiful things he was doing with his ravening lips, his tongue, his teeth.

It was as if he didn't hear. Her only answer came in the movement of his fingers toward a new goal. "No," she breathed. "Oh...!"

The words were barely audible, mere wisps of whispers that might have been low moans of delicious consent. Undeterred by them, Joshua's fingers began to fumble with the fastenings at her waist. Christy stiffened with deep shock, knowing she must not allow such liberties. As he began to slide the zip downward, for a moment she froze into stillness, afraid to move lest the gyrations of her hips drive either of them past the point of no return. She felt very close to something, tears or total response.

She cast her eyes about, desperately seeking some escape route. With the car light on anyone walking into the dim garage could hardly miss seeing. People in the house must have heard the car return. They might begin to wonder why Dr. Joshua was still in the garage. Anyone could walk in....

The shame of that imagined scenario helped Christy to conquer the worst of her sexual weakness.

At least the situation was such that he couldn't pos-

sibly take his romantic inclinations to conclusion. The
bucket seats in the Mercedes hadn't been designed for
the slaking of desires. It was safe, Christy felt, to challenge him with words—the only weapon with which she
could now extricate herself.

She glared at the top of his lowered head, striving for
anger to replace the glaze of desire. Her well-kissed lips
were still moist and tremulous, and tears of impotence
were stinging somewhere in her eyes, but she tried to
put defiance into the jut of her chin. Drawing on remembrance of what might have happened the previous
night in Joshua's bedroom, she flung a hurtful accusa-
tion at him. "You're so oversexed it's . . .*sick!*"

That brought his head jerking away from her breasts
and his hand from her waist. He threw back his head
against the headrest. His eyes were closed. Christy
could see the fierce grit of his teeth, the muscles moving
in the strong column of his throat, the pulse still throbbing in his temple. His throat worked for a few
moments, and then he groaned deeply as a hard shudder
passed through his body. It was as if some dark torment
had reached down into his very soul.

At last, with painful slowness, his eyes came open. He
looked down at her for a moment as though he didn't
quite comprehend.

"Let me go!" she pleaded. "What if someone were to
walk in?"

Some raw emotion touched his eyes. Wordlessly he
loosened his grip and freed her shackled wrist. Christy
didn't wait to hear if he had anything to say. Using her
trapped elbow and not particularly caring that it would
dig into a vital part of his anatomy, she levered herself
upward. She could hear him suck in his breath at the
sudden sharp pressure.

She sprang out of the car and slammed the door, then

stumbled toward the garage exit, trying to refasten her jeans and her shirt as she went.

She couldn't leave the garage in such dishabille, so she stopped to negotiate the brassiere fastening and the shirt buttons. Darkness made the task difficult and gave Joshua time to recover from the assault of her elbow. She was still working feverishly when he opened the driver's door, casting some brief illumination over the scene. She managed the last of her buttons, but in the same instant he caught up with her.

Hard hands captured her shoulders from behind, and the very touch of them seemed to rob her legs of strength. "Don't walk out now," he muttered in a cracked voice.

Safety gleamed beyond the door of the garage, where pale pools of light from the house fell onto the gravel driveway. But in the garage there was only darkness, and those masterful hands that had moved over her shoulders, and her own terrible weakness. . . .

His mouth buried itself in the soft cloud of her hair, murmuring her name into her ear with an urgency and passion that were matched by the way he pulled her close against his body. He was still supremely aroused. His heat and his height and his virility almost robbed her of the reason that she was struggling so hard to regain. Christy felt her willpower melting like warm wax as the palm of his flattened hand began to stir in slow, sensuous, comforting circles over the flat of her stomach. Try as she might, she could not wrench herself away.

"I wouldn't have forced you," he muttered thickly. His voice was low and ragged with emotion. "I promise I won't be so impetuous again. I do know how to be patient with a woman, how to wait. . . ."

His head was bending low into the hollows of her

throat. His hands slid persuasively over her shoulders, urging her softly back toward the car. He was handling her with care now, his touch infinitely tender despite the state of his need. His seductive gentleness pulled at her, enticed her, wooed her as force would not have done.

"We should talk this out. Come back to the car with me. Or we'll go down to the beach—it's private there. We can be alone...."

"No," she moaned, torn between her need to allow his hands their way and her need to escape. Sanity lay just a few feet away, but here there was only temptation....

"No," she groaned again, and made a choice for sanity. She wrenched herself away from his marauding hands and ran as if possessed by the devil himself.

5

In the end Christy did not phone David as planned. The events of the Sunday had been far too upsetting, and she knew her state of mind would communicate itself on the telephone. David would be sure to ask questions—questions she did not feel she could answer. David liked things laid out in black and white, and what was the black and white of this?

How on earth was she going to be able to continue in this job? A poor night's sleep, most of it spent wrestling with internal demons, offered no answer to the question.

During her restless tossing she gave almost no thought to the threat of firing that had preceded the lovemaking in the car, although she was conscious that Joshua Brent had meant every word. Whatever other faults her employer had, he was genuinely concerned for his daughter's welfare. If trouble continued, he wouldn't hesitate to act—and he would act in his daughter's best interests. Christy was certain that within a matter of days he was bound to become aware of the true state of affairs. At that point the person likely to suffer the ax was not her. But all this took very little mental energy, for in light of what had happened in the car speculation seemed pointless. It was fruitless to dwell on the prospect of being fired when she might very well decide to quit.

She had accused her employer of overly developed

sexuality, but in her heart she knew that part of the fault, during each of their encounters, had been her own wild and unreasoning responses. Something about him excited her unbearably, stirred her in sensual ways, woke sleeping fires deep in her core. He didn't even need to be touching her for the magnetism to be felt. Last night, even before Joshua Brent had pulled her against him, the awareness of him had been like fingers on her flesh. The very sight of his silvery ash hair and long gaunt body, even fully clothed, was evocative in the extreme. It was hard not to think of him intimately when her brain kept flashing erotic subliminal images of the nakedness she had viewed on the first day. In all her life she had never been so conscious of a man's virility—and of her own vulnerability....

Even thinking about the liberties he had taken caused her skin to grow damp and heated. His damnable attractiveness was at fault, of course. David's touch had never affected her in quite that way. But then David never persisted when Christy had called a halt to embraces. And Dr. Joshua had. She was well aware that his urgency and impatience could have been due to severe frustration. It was some months, after all, since his wife had died, and he had been an invalid during all that period with no chance to satisfy his normal male requirements. By this time, having sampled the extremity of his need, Christy was sure that Doris Moody must have been lying when she had hinted at a liaison.

All the same, was he so used to women falling beneath his spell that he didn't understand the word *no*? Several months of enforced abstinence didn't excuse such predatory behavior.

And even if Doris Moody had been lying, Christy was fairly sure that by this time the lie had become truth. Her own eyes had seemed to confirm it. Following the scene in the car, after an anguished hour of recovery spent in her own room, Christy had gone downstairs to eat the supper that had been saved for her in the kitchen. En route she had glanced along the hall that led to the other wing, her eye caught by a drift of movement. Doris had been wafting toward the door of Dr. Joshua's room, clad in a floaty black negligee. She had looked quite sure of her welcome, and Christy was also certain of the natural outcome. A man in a state of painful frustration didn't resist that sort of vision.

The knowledge didn't help Christy's insomnia. Her flesh crawled to think of what must be going on in that distant bedroom. And yet, she supposed she ought to be grateful to Doris Moody—thanks to her it might be possible to stay on in this job. Once satisfied in his needs, Dr. Joshua might actually stop behaving like a tomcat on the prowl.

Curiously, that thought gave Christy little comfort. Visions of twining limbs and tangling lips were not destined to solve the problem of her own acute frustration. Moreover, the ache of her leg muscles, a legacy of furious bicycle pedaling the previous day, was enough to remind her that females could get into a dangerous state of deprivation, too. All through the night she tossed and turned, thinking of what must be going on down the hall, and during most of those restless hours, she thought she would have to quit first thing in the morning.

She rose early, with the sun. Before seven she had showered and shampooed. The sight of her own nakedness was hardly reassuring, for she quivered to remember her vulnerability beneath Joshua's hands and the strong urges that had assailed her.

Oh, stop it, she told herself sternly as she pulled on a cheerful blue-and-green smock to face the new day. Of course she would stay. Natalie Brent needed her. How could she think of abandoning a retarded and perhaps disturbed child to the pernicious influence of a woman like Doris Moody? Surely for Natalie's sake she could conquer her sexual weaknesses!

She relieved some of her feelings by tugging a brush furiously through her newly washed hair, causing the short feathered cut to crackle and shine. For a long moment she stared into the mirror, willing her ordinary everyday face to undergo a metamorphosis. Perhaps more makeup would help. The nose was too short, she told herself critically. Would some carefully applied highlights help? The cheekbones were too wide, the skin too aggressively healthy. Should she try a pale foundation cream? The eyebrows were too level. Should she pluck them? The chin was too.... Oh, it was no good; nothing would make her beautiful, as she longed at this moment to be. What was the use? She had nothing to attract a man. Impatiently she pushed aside the contents of the makeup case and settled for a slash of bright red lipstick.

You haven't been hired to attract a man, she chided herself as she went downstairs on silent feet, so as not to disturb the sleeping household. *You've been hired to teach a child.* And this morning, thank goodness, the lessons would begin. It was nice to feel needed. Perhaps that was part of the problem: she had not been needed for these past few days, and it had given her too much time to indulge in self-analysis. Yes, it would be good to get to work. And as she was quite resolved to stay out of Doris Moody's way, there could be no more trouble of the kind that had developed yesterday.

Certainly there was no trouble at breakfast, for Christy had the kitchen to herself. Even Mrs. Cousins had not yet put in an appearance. By the time the housekeeper turned up, Christy had prepared her own breakfast and was cleaning up from it.

"Aren't you the early bird!" Mrs. Cousins's voice held a morning cheerfulness that told Christy here was a kindred spirit, another early riser. "I see you've already eaten. Well, I'm about to scramble some eggs for the rest of us. Although I suppose that won't do for Natalie. I wonder if she could manage French toast with jam instead of syrup?"

Christy hesitated, unsure of how much to tell Mrs. Cousins. She was loath to discuss the threat of her own firing, which might only embroil the housekeeper in a squabble that was best forgotten. On the other hand, she did not want the amiable Mrs. Cousins to do anything that might earn her, too, the wrath of Dr. Joshua. Finally Christy said carefully, "Perhaps it would be best if you didn't make a special menu for Natalie."

"Why, it's no trouble." But Mrs. Cousins stopped on the verge of cracking an egg over a bowl and looked at Christy with dawning suspicion. "That woman hasn't been making trouble, has she?"

Christy grimaced and saw she could not hide at least some of the truth. "Well, not for you. But it seems I interfered a little too much for her liking. So much for my smart-aleck responses! If you make French toast just for Natalie, Doris is sure to make another scene, and I don't think Dr. Joshua will take kindly to that."

"And I'm sure he shouldn't take kindly to the sort of scene that woman makes!" huffed Mrs. Cousins. Then she sighed and acquiesced. "All the same, you're right; there's no point in upsetting a semi-invalid. We'll leave Dr. Joshua out of this. I'll make French toast for everyone," she finished with a wicked little twinkle.

Christy laughed and poured herself another cup of coffee. "Don't be surprised if I vanish without drinking this," she remarked, settling back at the kitchen table. "When Doris arrives, I leave."

Mrs. Cousins shot a measuring glance over her shoulder. "That bad, is it?"

"Oh, not really. But discretion is the better part of valor. Or an ounce of prevention is worth a pound of cure. Or some such saying like that; I'm sure there's an appropriate one."

"How about 'let sleeping dogs lie'?" returned Mrs. Cousins in a malicious voice. "I expect she's jealous of you for having such an easy way with children. Honestly, that woman!"

"Sleeping cats is more like it," corrected Christy in a wry tone. "Anyway, it's best forgotten. Everything will blow over if I keep out of her way."

"Well, sit and enjoy your coffee for now. From the racket I heard upstairs, you won't be having to leave before you finish it."

"Oh?" Christy had heard nothing. The sounds of the far wing did not penetrate to the kitchen on the floor below.

"It's all about those shoes again," Mrs. Cousins explained. "Natalie just can't manage those laces—but she's not about to let that woman do it, either! The only thing fit to be tied right now is Mrs. Doris Moody—for I'm sure she doesn't want the doctor to see she's incapable of handling the child."

"Strange that Natalie should make such a fuss about it," said Christy reflectively. "I would have thought...." But then she halted in mid-sentence, deciding to keep her conjectures to herself.

"What's strange about it? Natalie doesn't like her nanny. It's quite clear to see, although the little one hasn't got the head to express herself vocally."

"I wonder!" smiled Christy. "She's expressing herself

vocally right now, from what you say! Maybe Dr. Joshua will get the message."

"I don't expect he will," sighed Mrs. Cousins. "As soon as he's on the scene, Natalie behaves like a dream, and so does you-know-who. Well, I expect I'd best stop dreaming myself," she finished, dropping a piece of egg-soaked bread into the frying pan, "and hurry up with the breakfast. Today's my day off, and Tom Maybee has offered to take me on a sight-seeing tour of the island. He has to go and pick up that bicycle anyway, and it seemed a good opportunity. I've left cold cuts and salad in the fridge for supper, and sandwiches for lunch, for I won't be home until late."

"Do I detect a blossoming romance?" grinned Christy.

"No!"

"All the same, I'm sure you've made a conquest," Christy said. "He seemed quite smitten the day you arrived."

"Oh, go away with you!" laughed Mrs. Cousins, turning crimson. "Tom Maybee is far too old-fashioned for me! For all that he's a nice man, he's right out of another century. Now stop your chatter, for I want to have this breakfast ready when the others come down. That child will be needing comfort when she arrives."

And indeed she must have needed it, Christy found herself reflecting some two hours later. Natalie had been given into her charge an hour before—a Natalie whose tear-bright eyes told of storms past but not forgotten.

The lessons were to take place in what was called the sunroom, a large, many-windowed, inviting space, sparsely furnished with shag carpets, simple chairs and a table. Everywhere were plants and bright pots of flowers that had been hastily carried in last week during the opening up of the house. Christy had brought, in her own suitcases, crayons and paintpots and books and various simple supplies, and although some of them had suffered in the accident on the ferryboat, there was enough to work with for a week or two at least. Yes, she had everything she needed.

Except Natalie's attention.... Looking now at the small girl lying faceup on the carpet, Christy cursed Doris Moody inwardly for the hundredth time that morning. Everything was wrong except the laces; *they* were beautifully tied. But Natalie's big purple eyes were staring into nowhere; the little fists were still clenched into tight knots. The corners of the small mouth had stopped trembling, but that was the only apparent sign of any improvement. And although Christy had spent the last hour reading aloud, or asking questions, or just chattering inconsequentially, Natalie had given no evidence of hearing a word. At last, hoping at least to gain the girl's trust for later lessons, Christy herself lay down on the shag carpet with a cushion under her head and gave in to silence, broken only by the occasional comment that she thought might stir Natalie's interest. And this was how Doris Moody found them at noon when she came to reclaim her charge.

"Well, I can see you're making lots of progress," said the auburn-haired woman tartly. "What were you teaching her—how to spell F-L-O-O-R?"

"No," returned Christy with a black glance that she could not resist, despite all threats of dismissal. "S-H-O-E-L-A-C-E. It seems to have taken up the whole morning."

Doris Moody's lips thinned dangerously. But perhaps she, too, had been told to avoid conflict. She scooped an unwilling Natalie off the floor without further comment and vanished in the general direction of the kitchen.

Despite gnawing hunger, Christy avoided lunch, deciding to eat later. But soon sounds of unhappiness from the kitchen warned her that the afternoon's lessons would be no more productive than the morning session had been. That realization only firmed her resolve to do something, and the sooner the better. She knew what she wanted to do: the plan had been formulated in her mind during the inactive morning. It was too bad that Old Tom was not around to give her a ride, but there were other ways to get about the island. Half a dozen bikes of assorted sizes still stood in the garage. Christy changed into a cool periwinkle-blue shirt and matching slacks that were somewhat more suitable for bike riding than the morning's smock; she ate a quick sandwich in the now empty kitchen and then she was ready.

Yes, Christy had a plan, but when her young pupil was once more delivered to the sunroom at two o'clock, she said nothing about it until after Doris Moody had left. Then and only then she turned to Natalie.

"All right, Natalie, lesson for this afternoon. We're going for a bicycle ride."

Natalie said nothing, but shook her head in vigorous denial.

"Oh. Hasn't anyone taught you how?" Christy felt a pang of disappointment, which was immediately replaced by optimism and renewed resolve. "We'll walk then," she said firmly. "We'll see more that way, and you can pick wild flowers, if you want, along the way. You might spot a field mouse, too."

Natalie didn't answer, but Christy thought she detected a gleam of interest in the purple eyes. It was enough encouragement that she caught Natalie's hand at once and started for the front door. In her haste, she nearly collided with Doris Moody in the hall.

"Where are you off to?" asked the other woman in a voice tight with suppressed annoyance.

"Out," said Christy with a fixed smile, about as communicatively as Old Tom would have done.

"Is that part of *lessons*?" came the belligerent reply. Doris still looked as if she were suffering the aftereffects of her past two hours with Natalie. She added acidly, "Or are you planning to save all the fun for study time and leave all the dirty work for me?"

A wicked imp beckoned; Christy could not resist. "Ayeh," she drawled in a deliberate and impudent use of the New England mannerism.

Doris Moody's face fell apart at the seams and then came together again in angry warning lines. "You'd better be planning to teach Natalie something this afternoon, or Dr. Joshua will hear about how little got done this morning."

Christy pasted a smile on her face. "Will you tell him why so little got done?" she said agreeably. "And don't worry, I am planning to teach Natalie something this afternoon, if I can. I-N-D-E-P-E-N-D-E-N-C-E. It may be a hard lesson, but it's worth learning. Shall I spell it out for you again?"

Doris's face became suffused with a dull red color. "Perhaps I'll speak to him anyway. And most certainly I will if you don't return from this little, er, outing by four-thirty. That's when I'm in charge again, remember?"

"I'll be back," returned Christy evenly. "Let's go, Natalie." And without waiting for an answer that might prolong the difficult scene, Christy bundled Natalie out the front door and down the steps. It wasn't until they were on the road into town, when she had had time to reflect, that Christy realized how much those few moments in the hall might cost her. This time, even Mrs. Cousins could not bear witness to what had happened. A moment's satisfaction—but had it been worth it?

Well, there was no point worrying about it now. The

main thing was to get Natalie into town and back again before the end of lesson time. It was a beautiful day today, and the walk seemed to be doing the child some good. The bloom was returning to her cheeks, and the sparkle to her eyes, as she ran ahead gathering reeds and wild flowers and generally running circles around Christy, who after yesterday was finding the distance tough going.

At length Natalie slowed somewhat and fell into step beside Christy.

"We're going into the town of Nantucket today, Natalie. You saw it the day you arrived. It's one of my favorite towns."

The purple eyes turned to Christy with a question written in them.

"We're going shopping," Christy elaborated. There followed a few moments of silence as the pair trudged along, and finally Natalie spoke the first word she had spoken to Christy all day.

"Why?"

"To buy you a pair of shoes without laces. Maybe two pairs, if we can find them in your size. Slip-on shoes. See the pair I'm wearing?" Christy demonstrated, kicking her foot out of a cork-soled sandal and sliding back into it at once, hardly missing a step.

"I *want* to tie laces," said Natalie stubbornly, to Christy's surprise. "I *will* tie laces."

Christy didn't let her amazement show and kept her voice matter-of-fact as she answered. "Of course you want to. We'll start learning how tomorrow morning, in lesson time. It's much easier if you start by tying bows that aren't on your foot."

"Mrs. Moody says your job is to teach me the alphabet," said Natalie suspiciously. "I don't like the alphabet."

"My job is to teach you anything you're ready to learn," returned Christy promptly. "The alphabet can wait. We'll start with laces and other things."

"What other things?" came the reply, scarcely less guarded than before. "Numbers? *She* said numbers and letters. She didn't say other things."

"What other things do you like?" countered Christy, now more than ever convinced that Doris Moody had been sowing seeds of distrust.

Natalie pondered a moment. "Music."

"Then we'll buy something today to make music with," Christy promised. "But we'll have to hurry or we won't have time. What's your favorite song?"

" 'Yellow Submarine.' "

"Maybe I'll teach you to play it, if we find the right instrument."

Christy, who had not forgotten her wristwatch today, was pleased to note a short time later that the walk into town had taken something less than an hour. Half an hour for shopping, she estimated; another hour for the return trip. And with luck they might spot the Jeep parked somewhere along the narrow streets and beg a ride home.

But it was not to be. There was no sign of Old Tom in town, nor of Mrs. Cousins. But Christy did have luck with other things. In a small shop she located a battery-operated toy organ with lettered keys—exactly the kind of thing she had hoped to find. Natalie might not like the alphabet, but Christy knew that a little incentive did wonders for the learning process. Then the shoes: two pairs were found, fitted and wrapped. It was time to get home.

They started on the road to Graydunes with an hour to spare. At first it seemed there would be no problem meeting the deadline, and the challenge thrown out by Doris Moody. But that was before the blister.

Oh, *no*, thought Christy, examining the watery swelling that had ballooned up on the side of her foot, with nearly a mile to go. The slip-on sandals were not her most comfortable. She had worn them primarily to give Natalie confidence in the idea; normally she would not have chosen them for walking. "It seemed like a good idea at the time," she muttered to herself, adding a silent curse.

And now the damage was done. Added to yesterday's legacy of aching muscles, the blister made walking a torture. Christy limped on, clutching shoe boxes and damning fate—and watching enviously as Natalie skipped blithely ahead. There had been no trouble lacing her back into her regular shoes for the return trip; she had been too enthralled by the toy organ she had been clutching in her hand . . . was still clutching in her hand, not wanting to let it out of her grasp for a moment.

And so it was that they arrived at Graydunes nearly half an hour late.

"You run on ahead, Natalie," Christy said as they reached the circular drive. Through the screen of trees, glimpses of Graydunes showed in the near distance. "Mrs. Moody will be waiting for you. I'll come along as fast as I can."

Which was not very fast, she reflected unhappily as she hobbled up to the front door some minutes after seeing Natalie vanish through it. Inside there was no sign of the child, or of the nanny. But a confrontation was waiting for her all the same, and even Doris Moody's unfriendly face would have been preferable to those cold gray eyes, and the long-legged figure that stood waiting with ominously folded arms. Joshua was angry, and Christy could feel his displeasure tingling all the way down to her blistered feet.

"Do you have any idea of the time?" growled the

voice that had such power to disrupt her. There were other disruptive things, too. His black pajamas, even when worn with a light striped dressing gown, had a way of conjuring up unsettling visions of what lay beneath their silky surface. And his pale hair, catching the sun from the skylight, was a reminder of the disturbing texture of him, which she could still see so clearly in her mind's eye. With effort she forced herself to concentrate instead on the glowering shadows of his eyes.

Finding pride an ally, Christy thrust her chin upward in a stubborn tilt. If he could pretend last night had never happened, so could she. "Yes, I'm late. I'm sorry."

"Too damn late. I was about to come looking for you again when Natalie came bubbling in the door. Today, I can't think that there's any excuse for you to vanish for the afternoon. I hired you to teach, Miss Sinclair, and I hear there's been very little of that going on, this morning or this afternoon." He looked pointedly at the parcels under her arm. "I can see for myself that it's true."

"Doris Moody has no idea why I went into town," returned Christy levelly, trying to maintain an even temper. "I had a very good reason. I was only—"

"I *know* about the shopping, Miss Sinclair. And Doris didn't tell me about that—Natalie did. Or don't you think she's bright enough to know where she's been taken?"

"Well, of course she is," said Christy, becoming angry. "Did Natalie tell you what we bought?"

"I heard about the shoes. And I saw the toy organ. Was that in the nature of bribery?"

"You can't believe that." Christy stared at him incredulously. "Why, the keys are lettered, and—"

"And of course that makes it all right," he broke in bitingly. "I'll admit it did me good to see Natalie's happy face when she came through that door. But it's bribery all the same. Doris is having quite enough trouble with Natalie as it is. She shouldn't have to compete with somebody who uses gifts to curry favor. And I hear you were very rude to her today—in front of Natalie, too. Do you deny that?"

"I wouldn't lower myself to deny it." Christy wrapped her arms tightly around the parcels in an effort to control the way her body was shaking with righteous indignation. "Now if you're quite finished, I'll tell you what I think about that woman's abilities with children. She's—"

"No, I'm not quite finished," he interrupted acidly. "I'm quite aware that this island isn't big enough to hold both of you. Perhaps there's some justice on your side, and if so, I'm willing to listen. But I won't have Natalie caught between two warring women. You must see that one of you has to go, and at once."

"Then it should be her," said Christy stubbornly. "She's doing Natalie no good at all. Ask Mrs. Cousins! You haven't given me a fair chance, and for your daughter's sake you should. I won't *let* you fire me without a fight."

"And a fight is just what I won't have. Now look, Miss Sinclair, I made Doris and Natalie hustle down to the beach for a swim so we could have this out in private. We have the house all to ourselves for the moment. If you have anything to say for yourself, say it now, for I'm quite willing to listen to your side. But I want it settled before they come back—and settled quietly. Now before you start in on your protestations, let me tell you that I'm willing to pay you for the entire summer. You have nothing to gain by creating a row, and nothing to lose by going quietly. You see, it's worth a lot to me not to have this house—and Natalie—disrupted anymore."

Somewhere early in his monologue Christy had let her chin fall to her chest, in order that her shaggy hair might curtain her eyes and the hurt in them. But now the chin came up, fighting and full tilt, and the hazel eyes held a sparkling challenge. "Is it really Natalie you're thinking of, Dr. Brent? Or is that...that *bitch* so much fun in bed that she's blinded you to her other faults?"

Perhaps she should have been more careful with her taunts, remembering how he had reacted to similar provocation the previous night. The fierce intake of breath warned her of his anger, but before she had time to take in the full import of his blazing eyes and thunderous brow his stride had covered the distance across the hall. His fingers dug into her shoulders, impaling her where she stood. The parcels in Christy's arms prevented any great closeness, and she clutched them as if they were a life buoy in a stormy sea.

"I said I was willing to listen to reason, not invective!" he rasped at her. "Do you always go on the attack like this by flinging unjust accusations? Is that the only way you can defend yourself?"

"I've said nothing that's untrue!"

"No?" he growled, the seething fury still just beneath the surface. "Last night your accusations were even more wild-eyed than they are today. I didn't take time to dispute them then, but I will now. According to you, I'm arrogant, lacking in fastidiousness and badly oversexed. D'you think I took pleasure last night in stopping when I did? Doesn't it occur to you that it took some effort to regain my self-control?"

"Are you suggesting you exercised *restraint*?"

"Considering the physical state I was in and the provocation I was subjected to—yes, I did!"

Christy gasped. "And I suggest you didn't! Any more

than you exercised restraint when Doris Moody went to your room last night!"

He started to shake with rage, and his fingers dug hurtfully into Christy's shoulders. "You try me sorely," he gritted out between his teeth. "The next time we're together I'll be damn tempted to prove to you exactly how much restraint I can use."

"There won't be a next time! You're firing me, remember?" She glared at him. "Will you please take your hands off me? Now that your sex life is attended to elsewhere you can start leaving me alone!"

"What the hell do you know about my sex life?"

"Let's leave sex out of this!" Christy cried, forgetting that she herself had inserted it into the conversation. Trembling beneath Joshua's hands, she was not being entirely logical. "Besides, I don't give a damn how you carry on with Doris Moody. That's not the point! She may be good at what she does with you, but she's not good at what she does with Natalie!"

"For a person who wants to leave sex out of the conversation you're damn obsessed with it!"

"So are you!"

Joshua's face was grim. "Perhaps I have been for the past few days. Do you have any idea what you *do* to me?"

"I know what *any* woman does to you! No wonder Doris succeeded!"

Storm clouds built in his eyes. His jaw tightened dangerously, and his next words were flung at her. "D'you really think I'd take a woman into my bed with my daughter sleeping in the very next room? Not Doris Moody, not *any* woman. I don't deny she came to my bedroom, and I don't deny the urge was pretty strong—especially after my unsatisfactory encounter with you. I'm no saint, and I've been subjected to more temptation than is good for a man. But dammit, Christy, give me some credit! I sent Doris away."

She stared at him, hardly able to believe he could have dredged up such willpower. For all her faults Doris was an experienced woman with blatant attractions, and she used them very obviously. Considering Joshua's physical condition the previous evening, he couldn't possibly have said no.

He seemed to understand Christy's disbelief. The ghost of a scornful smile curled the edge of his lips. "Oh, I'm not inhuman," he said sardonically. "Under more auspicious circumstances I would have been fair game. But Natalie sometimes has bad dreams. When she does, she comes into my room for reassurance. I hardly think it would help if she found her nanny in my bed."

Christy's eyes started to sparkle again, defiance returning as she reflected that Joshua's decision to let her go had indeed been influenced by Doris's obvious lures. The two of them deserved each other!

"Then you do admit you're attracted to her," she said tautly. "So it comes to the same thing, doesn't it? You want her in bed, so you're willing to turn a blind eye to her incompetence with Natalie while you wait for more auspicious circumstances to come along. Well, for your information, she doesn't have a clue about handling children. Perhaps you should hire her as your mistress instead! Natalie couldn't possibly be more bothered by having Doris in your bed than she is by having her in the nursery!"

Joshua bared his teeth with exasperation, and then his fury exploded. "Dammit," he thundered. "Don't you understand? I won't let sexual attraction for any woman cloud my judgment where my daughter is concerned. Good Lord, if I did, I wouldn't consider firing you. You fool, you blind little fool! Don't you know it's *you* I want to take to bed?''

They stood and glared at each other, angry silver eyes colliding with angry amber, until something dark and dangerous began to grow and smolder in the air between them like smoke rising to warn of a coming forest fire. It started with wisps of sensual knowledge and grew until the advancing heat of it could be felt in Christy's skin and in her blood and in her bones. In the darkening of Joshua's eyes and in the warm pressure of his hands at her shoulders she saw what was coming. When he started to pull her closer, her nerveless fingers released the one defense in her possession. The shoe boxes tumbled to the floor unnoticed. She knew she should run, and yet when his face descended, she remained rooted to the floor as if in a dream.

The anger he had expressed with his words could not be felt in his mouth, which moved over hers with gentle insistence, parting her lips with no need of force. She should have resisted—it was madness to submit to a man with whom she had just exchanged such angry words.

And yet it was a sweet madness, a magical madness, a madness that forced her reason to retreat, caused her senses to spiral and spin. . . .

His hands moved slowly over her shoulders, ranging the length of her, stroking the soft sensitive nape and then coursing downward to discover the contours of her waist and hips. He slid his fingers to the soft depression and cupped the slender curve of her buttocks, pulling her close against him. His persuasions were gentle, erotic in the extreme, no longer passionately predatory as they had been during their previous encounters.

Unreasoningly she succumbed to his male mastery. Her arms crept around him and her hands moved over his molded shoulders to feel the slide of loose fabric over warm well-muscled flesh. Drowning in a whirlpool of intoxicating sensations, she drank in the taste of him, her mouth asking for more than he gave. She was wanton where she should have been outraged, clinging where she should have been clawing, responsive where she should have been resistant. Mindless instinct told her to mold her body against his with willing softness, told her to touch his ears and thread her fingers in his hair. All the primitive woman in her leaped with triumph to feel the strong immediate response she provoked. She gloried in the intrusive depth of his kiss. Her arms moved around his neck and clung with passionate abandon, so that she had only herself to blame when he lifted her into his arms.

Christy was completely swept away by the dizzying ardor of the moment or she might have wondered from what deep source he had dredged up the strength for such exertion. Their mouths were still clinging hungrily when he carried her toward the upper landing, his hands compelling on her body and his tread slow and sure on the familiar stairs.

Unerringly he aimed for his own bedroom. With her eyes feverishly closed and her mouth thirsty on his, Christy was not fully aware of the direction he took. While she drank in the heady liquid aphrodisiac of his kiss, she heard a door kicked closed, felt herself laid on a bed, felt his weight and warmth come down alongside her in the same moment. His fingers ranged urgently over her curves, imperative in their movements. Her shirt was pulled free of her waist, and his warm hands slid upward beneath the fabric. And all the while his lips kissed her so commandingly she forgot all the reasons she shouldn't be submitting at all.

With her fingers twisting at his pajama collar she encouraged the beautiful things he was doing to her. She was vaguely conscious she was in his room, but it seemed of no particular importance. They could have been anywhere—a hotel room, an open beach. . . .

Driven to forgetfulness by the erotic fanning of his breath against her cheeks, she had little sense of time or place. All her being seemed concentrated in the purest of sensory responses. Against her hip she felt the powerful throbbing contours of his body and with some dim instinct knew he had leashed his own strong needs in order to arouse her gradually and fully, in proof that he was not always so aggressive in his demands.

Low in her throat, the involuntary purring and moaning competed with the heavy rasping sounds of Joshua's labored breathing. He was arousing her—but at some cost to himself.

He bathed her eyelids, her throat, her cheeks. And then his tongue and his teeth began nuzzling at an earlobe, exotic little licks and bites that caused her to gasp audibly and cry out at the sweet shock of sensation.

"Quiet," Joshua murmured against her skin. His hands were shaking with controlled urgency as they soothed her breasts and her hips, his voice so muffled and unnatural she could hardly have known he was talking, except for the hot fanning of his uneven breath and the press of his parted lips against her wildly sensitized skin.

The injunction for silence was enough to remind Christy that Natalie and Doris could return to the house at any moment. It was a tiny seed of reason, enough to bring her passion-drugged eyes open. . . .

She saw his head bending toward her, felt his velvet lips burn a trail down her neck. A brief hazy wondering about how those lips would feel moving over her entire body was not the route to rationality.

She tried to dredge up some shred of resistance from her disobedient body. If she didn't find strength to stop Joshua at once, soon nothing would. He was already fingering the clasp of her slacks. She moaned and twisted and put her palms against the flat of his stomach to stop him.

He must have misinterpreted her feverish movements. Growing impatient and no longer able to deny his own needs, he raised himself and threw off his dressing gown, then started to loosen the buttons of his pajama top. His face was darkened with obsessive passion, and his fingers had grown frenzied with haste.

And then Christy heard small distant sounds, barely audible in the thick-walled house...a door slamming, a child's wail, the tiniest echo of a woman's waspish voice....

She stared at Joshua with horrified realization as he started to pull the black fabric away from his shoulders. He seemed not to have heard the sounds from the lower hall. Driven by his particular demons, he was listening only to his own internal voices, the roaring of a great flash flood that approached too swiftly for escape.

"Stop!" she cried, and in one desperate movement she wrenched herself to one side.

In the same moment Joshua came heavily over her, his face consumed with a dark purgatory of desire. His arms closed around her, clamping her close. His body was still covered, with only the partial parting of his pajama front allowing her to feel the heat of his chest, which crushed heavily against her breasts. When she avoided his lips and tried to struggle away from beneath him, his head bent into her throat, his open mouth hot and avid on the tender curve. "Oh, God, let me," he moaned thickly. "You can't stop me now."

"Joshua, the others! They're here! You mustn't—"

He had not yet undressed, but he was past stopping, past listening, past caring. The minutes spent attending to slow and ardent stimulation had taken their toll, and his urgency had mounted far beyond the point of no return. Great shudders of need were traveling the length of his lean frame. She could hear him sucking in deep gulps of air, could feel the compulsive driven movements of his limbs. One long, tortured, guttural groan ravaged his chest, as if torn out of some terrible inner hell.

And then stillness.

He lay sprawled over her, absolutely motionless. She knew what must have happened. She was still stunned by the swiftness with which it had all taken place; not so many seconds had lapsed since the sounds of others arriving had come to her ears.

The house was now in silence, suggesting that Doris had probably taken Natalie to the kitchen for a glass of juice, perhaps in an effort to calm her down. The respite wouldn't last long. At any moment Natalie might come bursting up the stairs looking for her father, especially if she was in tears after some trying scene. Christy knew she must extricate herself from Joshua's arms—and very quickly, too. She started to squirm away from beneath him.

His arms tightened. "Don't you understand, Joshua?" Christy's voice was urgent. "I've got to get out of here!"

He had raised his head, and his eyes had come open. She thought she saw a brief pain flickering in their silvery depths. He rolled swiftly away and pulled a sheet over his legs. His mouth had become austere again, a change so swift it could not be fully accounted for by the slaking of passion. He started to button his pajama top, removing the scars from her sight. Hastily Christy left the bed and started to restore the disorder of her clothes.

While she fumbled her shirt back into her slacks Joshua

spoke. His voice was gruff. "I apologize for losing control—I didn't intend to touch you at all."

"I shouldn't have let things go so far," Christy said, shaken.

"Neither should I, under the circumstances. My only excuse is . . . ." He paused, and then his voice became decidedly curt and chilly. "I have no excuse. Please take my word for the fact that I normally have some self-control. I shouldn't have done that—but it doesn't alter any of my decisions. As I doubt I'll be seeing you again, I'll see you get a check before you leave in the morning."

Christy stared, hardly crediting the sudden change in him.

Seeing her expression, his mouth twisted cynically. "I did tell you I couldn't be swayed by sexual attraction," he reminded her dryly.

Christy gasped. "Surely you don't think I was responding simply in order to keep my job. You can't—"

"I don't think anything of the sort," he interrupted. Then, in a world-weary gesture, he ran ragged fingers through his pale hair. When he spoke again, his voice was considerably kinder. "I imagine you simply forgot yourself, just as I did."

Christy felt as if she had an obstruction in her throat. She was deeply disturbed by some difficult emotion she saw in Joshua's face, but she was also in a state of high apprehension lest others arrive on the scene. With shirt once more firmly tucked in place, she hurried to the door. Once she had reached it, she became less panicky. With Joshua a semi-invalid there were good excuses for holding interviews in his bedroom. She turned to face him, for pride demanded that she give some explanation for her lapses. She could not pretend she hadn't encouraged him during the first few minutes of lovemaking, even after finding herself in his bed.

She managed to keep her voice even. "Yes, I did forget myself. Completely, in fact. If I'd been thinking straight, I wouldn't have allowed any of this to happen."

Joshua smiled bitterly. "But you thought straight partway through, didn't you? When you saw what you had let yourself in for, you couldn't go through with it. And perhaps it's just as well. I'd have had a hell of a time letting you go if things had reached a natural conclusion." He frowned and glanced away briefly, as if unwilling to admit that for himself the conclusion had been very natural indeed. When he looked at Christy again, his face had become a mask, his eyes unrevealing. "My scruples would hardly permit firing a woman right on the heels of making love to her. Perhaps it's as well you were shocked into stopping."

Christy placed her hand on the doorknob, ready to leave. "If you'd heard Natalie come through the front door, you might have been shocked into stopping, too," she said urgently. "Now excuse me, I have to go."

On the instant his eyes turned icy. "Must you invent excuses? I'm quite aware of the repugnant thing that made you change your mind."

Christy had slipped through the door and was halfway along the hall before she realized he meant his scars.

6

CHRISTY STARTED TO PACK her possessions at once, with a heart like a millstone. Surrender. Utter, abject, humiliating surrender.

How could she possibly stay after what had happened? Her near capitulation was warning enough she shouldn't contemplate remaining within Joshua's reach. She thought she would never again be able to look him straight in the eye. It didn't help her state of mind to realize his reaction to her was not unique. He had claimed to be attracted to Christy—but he hadn't denied his attraction to the seductive vision that had appeared in his bedroom the previous night.

As far as her job was concerned, Christy felt she ought not to have surrendered. Natalie needed her and would need her more and more as time went on, when Doris Moody's harmful influence began to make itself felt. She knew, too, that Mrs. Cousins could be enlisted in her defense—would probably spring to her defense when she became aware of what was happening. As things stood, however, it was unlikely that the housekeeper would have an opportunity to state her point of view before Christy left on the morning ferry.

Yes, Christy knew she could have fought Doris Moody and probably won. Surely Joshua would be able to see reason if he understood the full facts of the case. He had his daughter's welfare at heart. In the normal way, Christy was sure, he would not have been led astray by a woman like Doris Moody—despite her very obvious sexual attractions. But as a semi-invalid, Dr. Joshua had seen little and heard little of what was going on in the household. He had been subjected to only one side of the story. He had indicated his willingness to hear the other side, but now Christy did not want to tell it.

Yes, she could have fought Doris Moody. But she could not fight herself, and she could not fight her own attraction for Dr. Joshua Brent. It had been there from the beginning, she realized now, for him as well as for her—an awareness that ran like a high-tension wire between them. Not love. Love was something that took time to develop; love was the reassuring companionable relationship she had with David. This was a drive far more primitive and basic, something she had recognized at first sight of the man and then yesterday admitted freely to herself. Sex. Sex. S-E-X. A violence of feeling that made her fear for what might happen if she stayed here. It was best to go while it was still possible to go without scars.

The sounds of nanny and child coming upstairs were muffled by the relatively soundproof walls of the house. But Natalie's howls of outrage, soon after, were not. Shoelace time again, thought Christy grimly, remembering the two boxes that had tumbled unheeded to the floor in the hall. Later tonight she would retrieve them and put them outside Natalie's door. Perhaps they would be found in time to stop the morning scene.

But when the howling continued unabated for another ten minutes, Christy could stand it no more. Resolving to brave whatever encounter might come of her interference, she left her bedroom and started toward the stairs. But as she reached them, the howling miraculously hiccuped to a halt. She listened for several minutes and heard nothing. She went down the stairs and retrieved the spilled parcels, then came back up the carpeted flight. At the head of the stairs she stood uncertainly, looking down the empty corridor. . . .

And Joshua emerged from Natalie's room. Christy wheeled away.

"Christy, wait! Don't run away from me. For God's sake, woman—" And in several strides he had reached her side as she scurried back toward the safety of her own room. He caught her shoulder just as her free hand reached for the doorknob, and the movement whirled her around to face him.

"Why didn't you tell me?"

"Tell you what?" Christy's face felt as if it would crack with the effort of showing nothing. She longed to escape, but with his fingers digging patterns into her arm she could do nothing but stand and listen.

"About what's in those parcels you're holding."

"But you already know. Natalie told you. You said—"

"I know now. But I didn't know everything before. She hadn't told me who the shoes were for. She was too excited about the other, the toy— Dammit, Christy, why didn't you tell me your side of the story? Don't you know Natalie was in there howling for *you*? Doris wasn't getting anywhere with her, so I finally went in and found out the truth. Natalie wants her new shoes."

"Well, here they are." Christy pushed the boxes in his direction, but he shook his head and refused to take them.

"You'll have to give them to her yourself. You paid for them, didn't you?"

Christy nodded, and was relieved that he did not add insult by offering to reimburse her.

"She's all right for now; I tied her laces." Joshua's hand still restrained her, preventing her from entering her room. "Why didn't you tell me—or don't you have the normal instincts of self-defense?"

"Of course I do, but— Oh, what difference does it make?" she finished with a queer hollowness in the pit of her stomach, and made efforts to shrink away from his hand.

"All the difference in the world, and you know it, Christy. I'm beginning to think you were right—I have been blinded. By *you*. I've been so damn afraid of letting my attraction for you interfere with my judgment that I've gone too far in the other direction, and— Why on earth are you looking at me like that?"

"Because you're touching me, Dr. Brent," Christy said, trying to conceal the tremor in her voice. She addressed him formally, a small weapon to combat the disruptiveness of his presence and the memory of the intimacy they had shared. "I am an engaged woman, after all. I may have forgotten it for a few minutes this afternoon, but I don't intend to forget it again."

His fingers fell away, as if stung, and his voice turned as formal as hers. "I apologize. All I'm trying to say is that I would prefer you to ignore what I said earlier." He added stiffly, "I want you to stay."

Christy steeled herself to remain cool. "I really don't want to now."

A muscle worked in Joshua's jaw. With a small sense of surprise Christy realized this encounter was even harder for him than it was for her. It was the first time she had considered his possible embarrassment about the scene in his bedroom. And yet, having considered it, she knew with a certainty that it must have taken a great swallowing of male pride for him to approach her like this.

"Because of what happened?" he asked quietly.

"Yes," Christy said, and their eyes met and held for

one difficult moment as the memory of the afternoon's passion hung in the air between them.

A proud closed look shuttered Joshua's face and he moved farther away, putting space between them. She knew he was thinking of the scars again, believing she had found them repellent. She could think of no way to disabuse him without admitting to her strong physical attraction. And that she couldn't do.

His voice was very controlled. "If you think I intend to repeat the scene, you're mistaken. I'm not proud of what happened—surely you must realize that. Please understand that I'm asking you to stay for Natalie's sake, not for mine."

"It's no good," Christy said, shaking her head. At the moment she felt an urgent need to get back into the sanctuary of her own room, away from his compelling presence, away from this conversation that seemed to have taken too personal a turn. "It won't work. And Doris will get along better without me here. I upset her because . . . because I don't have trouble with children. If she doesn't feel threatened, she may improve."

"Doris Moody is in her room packing," he returned in a dry tone.

Christy stared at him in astonishment. "You mean you've fired her? Just like that?"

He frowned. "I didn't exactly fire her. She'd been promised a summer's employment, and despite her difficulties with Natalie she seems very eager to please. I'm sending her to New York. I share offices with several other doctors, and it happens there's a temporary opening—our regular receptionist is away for several weeks this summer. God knows, Doris is decorative and charming enough, and she'll be better at that than— Oh, dammit, Christy, can't you forget about my lapses?" His lean fingers raked the ash-blond hair, and his face appeared troubled. "Stay and help Natalie. You must want to, or you would have agreed to take the money and run. If you go, Natalie will have nobody."

"She'll have Mrs. Cousins," protested Christy, feeling trapped, "and you. And you can hire another nanny."

"Mrs. Cousins has quite enough to do with a household this size. And yes, I can hire another nanny—I intend to, in fact. But I can't hire another teacher. And Natalie needs those lessons. You know she does. Don't let her down. She *needs* you."

"Needs you." The words were like a brand in Christy's brain. But she had her own needs to consider, and she hated him momentarily for making this so difficult for her. All the same, her hand faltered on the doorknob, and her uncertainty must have been apparent, for he went on convincingly.

"Who else will teach her to play 'Yellow Submarine'? Natalie told me you promised. And to tie shoelaces? You see, we had a short talk after I sent Doris Moody back to her rooms and calmed Natalie down. She told me quite a lot of things in those few minutes."

"Oh, please," pleaded Christy, "you're making this very difficult for me."

"And I intend to," he returned grimly, "for I can't have you leaving now."

"And I can't stay. I don't deny that I'd like to help Natalie, but under the circumstances—"

"Would it help if I promised?" he broke in.

"Promised what?"

"Promised never to touch you again."

"Well...."

"Then I promise," he went on quickly without waiting for her verdict. Then, running a hand through his hair again, he exploded, "Oh, damn, I can't promise the impossible. Let me put it this way. I'll never touch you again except with your prior approval."

Decisions chased each other through Christy's head. Joshua Brent seemed like a man who would keep a promise; and surely when she saw David again things would fall back into perspective. Even so, it would be hard, she thought to herself: how hard, only time would tell. But Joshua's promise, and his apologies, made it nearly impossible to refuse his request. And as he had pointed out, she, too, had made promises—to Natalie. And she wanted to keep those promises.

It wouldn't be easy. If Joshua had taught her one thing during these past few days it was that she was exceptionally vulnerable where he was concerned. He might have promised not to touch her with his hands, but he could still touch with his voice, with his eyes . . . most of all with his eyes. There was something about the way he looked at her, even now when he was trying to be politely dispassionate, that caused her stomach muscles to tense and tighten into hard peculiar knots.

Again her hand found the security of the doorknob. "Then I have another condition to add," she said.

"What condition? Don't make it an impossible one," he warned.

"Don't hire a nanny. I'll look after Natalie myself, starting in about fifteen minutes, with suppertime." She opened the door and backed into her room. "And please. . . ."

"Please what?" he prompted when she hesitated.

"Stop looking at me like that," she exclaimed testily, closing the door between them.

THE DAYS THAT FOLLOWED were not as difficult as Christy had supposed they might be. With Doris Moody in New York, the household settled into a comfortable routine.

Old Tom Maybee tended his roses; Mrs. Cousins tended her kitchen; Christy tended and taught Natalie.

As to her engagement, Christy's feelings were very much in limbo. She knew something must be badly awry when she responded with such intense abandon to another man. She began to wonder whether she had simply drifted into the arrangement with David, perhaps as a form of armor against other importunate males. She had never wanted to hop into bed without commitment—something many men of her generation seemed to expect as a matter of course. As the engagement had been largely a long-distance thing—Christy in Boston, David in Baltimore—it was quite possible that her subconscious had made a choice that was based in part on self-protection. She hated to think she might have been using David like that, but she was beginning to wonder if it was the case.

She realized she would need to see her fiancé again before reaching deeper decisions. And in the meantime she would try to put thoughts of Joshua into cold storage. At night, however, erotic dreams came to plague her. There were tormenting visions of marble-hard smoothness, disturbingly dusted with ashen crispness— but that could be pure frustration, as she had recognized from the start. . . .

She had other reactions to Joshua that were even more difficult to deal with, reactions based on the man she gradually discovered him to be. Much as she tried to stay out of his path, awareness of him increased as day followed day. Even when she didn't see him his strong personality permeated the house. Many things—his firmness in dealing with minor household problems, his small kindnesses toward Mrs. Cousins, his attachment to his daughter, his dry sense of humor, even his touch of male arrogance—attracted her in ways that had nothing to do with sex. But she couldn't allow herself to fall in love when she was still engaged to another man.

She felt unsure and troubled about these things, and so matters remained in suspension. A phone call to David did nothing to resolve them. She had already told him, in a letter written shortly after her arrival, about some other members of the Graydunes ménage. There had been only one notable exception, and David brought it up on the telephone.

"How about your employer? Is he still in hospital?"

"Er, no, David. He decided to spend the summer here, on Nantucket, with his daughter."

"I thought he was supposed to be in pretty bad shape."

"He was, but he's over the worst. He needs more plastic surgery, but it's strictly cosmetic now. He's badly scarred."

"Not that I wish him ill," teased David, "but better that than a handsome devil."

"The scars aren't on his face, David."

"Oh." There was a pause. "Is he good-looking?"

"Well, as a matter of fact he is, quite."

"Rich? He must be rich."

"Yes— Oh, David, you're not going to be jealous, are you? He's *much* older than me, and quite short-tempered at times." Well, that was true as far as it went, wasn't it? "Frankly, he's a little overpowering."

"I take it you don't like him."

"I avoid him as much as possible," Christy said, letting a twist of the truth serve as answer. The phone call ended without further incident, and it was only after she hung up that she realized she had not mentioned that she was now fulfilling the function of nanny as well as teacher.

Joshua seemed absolutely determined to maintain an

impersonal relationship between them, just as she was. Although he spent far less time confined to his room as the days progressed, he spent very little of it in Christy's presence, except when others were around. As he gained strength, he took Natalie under his own care for increasing periods of time each day. He would vanish with his daughter on outings that Natalie would sometimes describe later for Christy. The Whaling Museum, Hilltop Stables, the Observatory, the Old Mill, Sankaty Lighthouse—it seemed that Joshua was determined to introduce his daughter to the island where he had been born, and occasionally Christy found herself wishing almost wistfully that she had not been excluded.

Most of the time, however, it seemed that Joshua took Natalie off to secluded beaches where they would swim and explore the rocky shore for an hour or two. That this was so was apparent not only from information gleaned from Natalie, but also from Joshua's changing appearance. He was far more relaxed, looked healthier and had even lost some of his pallor. But if he spent a good deal of time swimming and walking, he spent none of it at the private stretch of beach belonging to Graydunes. Was it to avoid her company, Christy wondered, or to avoid displaying his scars? Instinctively she knew that the truth lay somewhere between. Time had probably blurred the outlines of those harsh red weals on his torso; certainly they would be less painful by now. But without further plastic surgery, they would always be there.

Natalie's lessons were going well. The tying of laces had at last been conquered—not easily, but the child's determination to learn had helped. And with tunes translated into letters of the alphabet, Natalie was discovering, painstakingly, how to recognize at least those letters on the keyboard of the toy organ. As she grew to trust Christy more and more, she also grew more communicative. And as she grew more communicative, a suspicion grew in Christy's mind, and gradually the suspicion became a certainty.

Christy did not believe that Natalie Brent was retarded at all.

True, there were simple things the child could not cope with. But Natalie was alert enough in other ways, although her alertness must have often been concealed by her reluctance to open up to strangers. And Christy had to agree with Joshua that Natalie's problems were not emotional, despite the fact that the child would often dissolve into tears with sheer frustration—and then, for a time, the whole learning process would grind to a noisy and upsetting halt.

"Let's make a letter," Christy had suggested once, picking *A* because it happened to be on the keyboard of the organ. "Look...like this." And she had drawn a large capital letter for Natalie to copy. "Trace it if you like."

"I can't," Natalie had demurred, refusing to take the felt marker that was handed to her.

"You know that letter, Natalie. I know you do!"

"It's an *A*," came the answer, "but I can't make it."

"Yes, you can. Try. Then, when you've done it, I'll show you the new tune I worked out for you last night."

So at last, with that incentive, Natalie had taken the felt marker in her hand and tried. The *A* that resulted had not been such a very bad *A*—it was vaguely recognizable—but Natalie's storm of tears had been swift and violent and unexpected. She was far too upset to hear compliments for her effort, and it was some time before Christy was able to soothe her.

Despite the feeling of exhaustion that always followed that kind of emotional upheaval, Christy was, in a way, not displeased. Natalie had the intelligence to be frustrated; she knew she had not made a good *A*. A less intelligent child would have been satisfied with the effort; Natalie was not. So Christy reasoned that whatever was interfering with the learning process, it was not lack of intellectual capacity. If Natalie had been properly tested and instructed three years earlier, she might be reading already.

But for the time being Christy kept her counsel and continued to make her observations. If only she had had more experience with this type of child! If what she suspected was true, there were ways to teach a girl like Natalie. But Christy's experience had been along quite different lines, and at best she could only try to remember some of the things she had heard. As yet she was not prepared to alert Joshua to the possibility of what she was coming to believe.

But she made large letters out of fuzzy felt and textured papers and asked Natalie to trace them with her fingers, over and over again. On the clean stretch of Graydunes beach she tramped big letters in the sand and had Natalie follow in her footsteps. She started to trace letters with her finger on Natalie's spine, asking her to guess which letters they were, and making a game of it. In turn, Natalie would trace the same letters on Christy's spine—something that never resulted in tears, for Natalie could not see visible proof of her mistakes.

And everything Christy learned only served to confirm her initial suspicions. Natalie was clever enough—and at times too clever by half!

"Why don't you get along with my dad?" came the disconcerting observation one Monday in late July, when Christy had been on Nantucket for more than five weeks. It was a warm, but rather cloudy day, and the schoolroom had been abandoned in favor of the beach and bathing suits and tracing letters on bare spines.

"I do get along with your dad. But you're changing the subject, Natalie. We were making letters. Don't think you can get out of it so easily! You were going to do an *N* on my back—*N* for Natalie."

Natalie obliged with a backward *N* and then said, "There, it's done. Now you have to answer *my* question, Christy."

"What question?" Christy forced a light laugh, although she knew perfectly well what Natalie meant. "In any case I did answer it."

"*You* can't get out of it, either, Christy," said Natalie stubbornly.

"What on earth is that supposed to mean? Now come on, Natalie—a letter *A*."

"I won't do an *A* until you've told me why you don't get along with my dad."

"Whatever gives you the idea that I don't? We're always perfectly civil to one another."

"You never look at each other." And before Christy had time to formulate a reply to that, Natalie plunged on, "Well, except sometimes. And never at the same time. If he's looking, you're not. And if you're looking—well, then, you look at him as if, as if . . . ."

"As if what? There's nothing strange about the way I look at your dad." This was one of those moments when Christy was regretting Natalie's growing loquaciousness. "Now let's get back to letters."

"Yes, there is," Natalie persisted. "As if you were afraid to touch him."

"Natalie, that's nonsense! I'm not afraid to touch him."

"Why do you stay so far away from him, then? As if . . . as if you thought he was going to burn you? I think my dad would *like* you to touch him. Probably just to see what it feels like."

"Natalie!" Christy's sense of shock was not at all pretended. How had the child been so observant? "Of course he doesn't want me to touch him."

"Why not? People touch," observed Natalie philosophically. "You should do it, and then you'll stop thinking about it, and so will he. He wouldn't do anything to you. Mrs. Moody used to touch him all the time, whenever she thought she could get away with it, and he didn't do anything to her. Even though she pretended he had."

So that little scene in the kitchen, so long ago, had not gone over the girl's head.... Well, it only confirmed what Christy had come to feel about Natalie's native intelligence. But at the moment Christy could only wish that Natalie did not have quite so much of it. She was glad her eyes were still turned to the sea, and that Natalie was behind her back.

"Your dad wouldn't like you to talk about people touching him," Christy said with a firmness that was entirely manufactured. "I'm still waiting for that letter *A*."

"Why wouldn't he?"

"Because— Oh, look, Natalie, there's a quahog shell."

"Why wouldn't he?"

"Because...touching between grown-ups is a special kind of thing. It means affection. You save it for the people you really care about, at private times. If grownups go around doing too much touching, it loses its meaning."

"I guess my mother felt that way, too," returned Natalie calmly, with no idea of the mixed and very grown-up reactions her words were causing. "She didn't touch much at all. Not even me. My dad always liked cuddling, when I was little, but she didn't. She didn't like touching."

"She...." But the small sense of shock was replaced immediately by the need to say something that would sidetrack Natalie. Christy did not feel she could continue to listen to such disturbingly intimate observations. Deciding directness might have some merits, she went on crisply, "She probably saved it all for private times. Now, Natalie, I don't want to talk about that anymore. Let's go for a swim."

"I don't want to swim." Natalie could be quite mulish when she wanted to; and this, unfortunately, was one of those times. "And I know why you don't want to talk. You think I don't understand about grown-ups touching. But I do—my mother explained it to me. About the seed and everything. She believed in being honest about things like that. Don't you?"

Christy heaved a deep sigh and gave in to the inevitable. "Yes. Yes, Natalie, I do. I won't try to change the subject again."

"Good." Natalie settled back, content with her small victory. "Then maybe you'll tell me why you're afraid to touch my dad. I don't mean grown-up touching. Just touching. Even Mrs. Cousins touches him sometimes, when she hands him something, or when he helps her into a coat."

"I told you, Natalie, I'm—"

"But you *are* afraid," Natalie contradicted. "If he walks into a room, you walk to the other end of it. If he passes the salt at dinner, you wait until he's put it down on the table before you pick it up. Once I saw you bump into him, and you jumped right away. Is it because you don't like him?"

"Of course not. I like him perfectly well."

"Then why?"

"Oh, Natalie, you're making this difficult! I suppose it's because I'm afraid he might touch me back again."

"Grown-up touching."

"Yes," admitted Christy unwillingly, "grown-up touching."

"Well, that's a relief." Natalie let out a small contented sound. "I feel better about it now. I was afraid you hated my dad. Now I know it's only that you like him too much."

"Natalie, I *don't*," protested Christy with a distinct sense of entrapment.

"Don't what?" came a deep voice from behind both their shoulders, and Natalie jumped up at once, making sounds of delight.

Christy skimmed a quick glance behind her—long enough to see a pair of muscular legs covered with a pale dusting of hair, and Natalie's slender frame being hoisted on high. Beyond that she saw nothing, for she turned her eyes away at once, not daring to let her own alarmed expression be seen.

"Never mind answering," came that voice again, and there was mockery in it. "I heard. Christy doesn't hate me, but on the other hand she doesn't like me too much."

"That's not it at all," Natalie protested. "You didn't hear the whole conversation."

Thank heaven for that, Christy breathed in a silent prayer—but then wondered exactly how much he had heard. Nothing else, she hoped.

"Oh, I heard a little," came the disconcertingly casual reply, shattering the hope. "You were talking about touching."

"Christy's afraid of touching," said Natalie with alarming forthrightness. "She shouldn't be, should she?"

"Oh, Natalie," interjected Christy with growing despair, "I didn't exactly say that."

"Yes, you did exactly say that." Natalie relinquished

her grasp around her father's neck and dropped back to the sand. "And you also said—"

"I'm sure Christy doesn't want to go through the whole conversation all over again," Joshua broke in easily, sparing Christy the embarrassment of a complete recapitulation. All the same, her face mirrored her consternation, and she was glad the others remained behind her back, closer to the hummocks of grass. Joshua went on, "I've come to take you for a swim, Natalie. Christy's had your company all day. Now it's my turn."

"Why does it have to be anybody's *turn*? Why can't we all swim together?"

Joshua ruffled his daughter's dark hair and laughed. "Christy needs a break, pet. From *you*. You've turned into a regular chatterbox this summer, d'you know that? At times, anyway."

"Christy doesn't mind me talking," Natalie stated, although there was a little worry in her voice. "She likes it."

"That's because she's a good listener. But she can't listen all the time, can she? She'll wear out her ears. Now fetch your towel, Natalie, and let's go."

"I'd rather stay here," replied Natalie, and her little streak of stubbornness took over. She dropped to the sand beside Christy and dug her toes in. "*You* don't mind if we stay, do you, Christy?"

Christy put a brave face on the only possible response she could make. "Of course not."

"Well, then." Natalie's voice was triumphant. "Besides, we haven't finished our game."

It appeared Joshua was ready to give in, for he came and lowered his long frame to the sand beside Natalie. Now, with those powerful limbs in the corner of her vision, Christy could see that he wore fawn-colored bathing trunks and a beige T-shirt. An old fisherman's hat covered most of his face and she was unable to read the expression in his eyes as he gazed in her direction. He was still gaunt, Christy thought—but muscular and virile, too. Her heart seemed to skip a beat.

"What game?" he asked, letting loosely crossed arms fall over his bent knees. "Can I play—or will it be too hard for me?"

"Of course not!" exclaimed Natalie, without waiting for Christy's response. "All you have to do is write letters with your finger, on Christy's back."

There was a moment of awkward tension—a tension that stretched between Christy and Joshua without including the child who sat between them, although she may have noticed it.

Joshua spoke softly, breaking the bond, and his meaning was clear—to Christy, at least. "I think that would be too hard for me, Natalie."

"Oh, dad, don't be silly!"

"I'm not being silly," returned Joshua soberly. "Hard for me—and hard for Christy. Didn't you say she's afraid of touching?"

Natalie looked from one to the other of the grown-ups beside her, disappointment and anxiety clouding her beautiful purple eyes. "But Christy says you stop being afraid of things if you try them. Don't you, Christy? That's what you say if you want me to try things."

What could she say—what was there to say? Several weeks of determined effort had brought Natalie a long way. The child had opened up, become more responsive and less afraid of trying new ventures. But it was a fragile beginning, based largely on trust, and in the company of others, except her father, Natalie still went back into the cocoon that had protected her from failure for so many years.

Christy had already decided on her answer when

Joshua added casually, "There's another thing, Natalie. I made a promise not to touch Christy. Now I can't break that, can I?"

"It's only a game!" declared Natalie.

"Of course it's all right, in this case," said Christy quickly. "I release your dad from his promise. Finish spelling your name and show your father how it's done. You only did the *N*."

Christy shifted her position, turning her spine to Natalie. A small finger traced the remaining letters.

"That was very good," came Joshua's voice. Christy could hear the amazement in it, only partially concealed. She knew he had been unaware of how far Natalie had progressed in the past few weeks. To him Natalie's abilities would come as a complete surprise. Natalie still could not read, or at least could read almost nothing. As for printing letters on paper, there were very few she would even try. But she could spell many words, and Christy knew she could not take the credit for that. In those years of school Natalie had absorbed far more than had been suspected. Because she lacked some abilities, it had been assumed that she did not have others. Now, as the child's confidence increased, she was showing what she could do.

"Do another word, Natalie," Christy urged. "Your father wants to see you do more. This time I'll guess."

Natalie's finger started once more on its task.

"Joshua," Christy said. "You spelled Joshua."

"That's great, Natalie! I didn't know you could do my name. Can you do Christy's?"

"If I did, then there'd be nothing to guess," declared Natalie. "This time *you* can guess what I'm writing on Christy's back, dad—by watching me." She started another word.

"Do that one again," said Joshua in an offhanded voice a few moments later. "I missed part of it."

"Did I do it wrong?" asked Natalie anxiously.

"Not at all," replied her father. "You did it far too fast! I turned my head away for just a second, to stop a sneeze, and it was all over."

Natalie was partly content with that explanation. Christy knew why Joshua had asked for the repetition. She prayed he would guess correctly this time.

"You spelled Brent," he said casually, and well-hidden relief flooded Christy, for most of the letters had been written backward, and one upside-down. "You're full of surprises, aren't you, Natalie?"

"Oh, Natalie can spell a lot of words," Christy told him, turning back to face the others. "You would be surprised." Her eyes caught Joshua's; the secret was out.

"Sometimes I can't print them on paper, though," Natalie told her father with a return of anxiety, "or tell the words when I see them."

"You will, soon enough," said Christy easily. "Haven't I told you people are clever at different things? Your dad is clever at doctoring. You're clever at spelling and music."

"And you're clever at reading," came the morose reply. "I wish I could read."

"Some people have to work harder at some things, that's all," Christy encouraged her. "In your case it's reading. In my case it's writing—I always had trouble because of being left-handed. Everybody has to work hard at something."

"Christy's right," Joshua interjected. "We all had problems once. Mine used to be spelling."

"But you're good at most things," Natalie said in a discouraged tone—the kind of tone Christy had been contending with for much of the summer. "I have to work hard at everything. I've been trying for weeks to learn to tie laces, and I still don't do it quite right."

"You do it quite right enough." Christy kept her voice cheerful. "And you don't find everything difficult. Look how well you play tunes now! I've been meaning to tell your father you should have piano lessons."

"What a good idea! Christy's quite right," Joshua agreed seriously. "You won't have to work hard at *everything*, Natalie. You weren't born on a Saturday, you know."

"Saturday? What does Saturday have to do with it?" Natalie looked at her father questioningly. The corners of her mouth, which had started to turn down a moment ago, now betrayed some curiosity, and Christy blessed Joshua for distracting the child's attention from her own failings.

Joshua pretended astonishment. "Surely you've heard that old nursery rhyme: 'Saturday's child works hard for a living.' And you, of all people, born on the very best day of the week! Don't tell me you don't know the words."

"Yes, I know them," claimed Natalie, and rattled off the rhyme to prove her knowledge. She concluded, quite cheered by the thought, "Was I born on a Sunday?"

"Yes, you were," her father told her. "There's no better day than that. Now I was born on a Wednesday." He made a woeful face.

Natalie laughed delightedly and turned to Christy. "What day were you born, Christy?" she asked.

"I don't know," Christy smiled. "I suppose I was told once, but I've forgotten. So I'll just pick a day for myself! I'll take Monday, because that's what it is today."

"Monday's child is fair of face," Joshua inserted lazily.

"Monday doesn't suit you," said Natalie, cocking her head to one side and then adding, with the devastating honesty of a young child who has not yet learned deceit, "You're sort of pretty, but you're not pretty enough for Monday."

"I think she's quite pretty enough," Joshua drawled, his lids half-closed as he contemplated the object of Natalie's observations. "But you're right, Natalie; there's a day that suits Christy better. I think she must have been born on a Friday."

Christy knew he intended it as a compliment even before Natalie's voice piped up with the reminder, "Of course! Friday's child is loving and giving. *That's* Christy's day."

The great warmth of Joshua's eyes had nothing to do with sexual attraction: nor were his words intended to be suggestive in any way. He was telling Christy he understood how much she had done for Natalie with the simple tools of concern, caring and attentiveness. It was the most he could say in Natalie's presence.

Christy felt her face grow slowly crimson, for the gray eyes meeting hers over Natalie's head had still not turned away, and the look in them spoke worlds. To cover her embarrassment, she jumped to her feet and said briskly, "Anyone for a swim? If I don't get wet soon, I'm going to burn to a crisp!"

"Yes, your face is already quite pink," observed Joshua with high amusement—a comment that drove Christy to run to the water immediately, without looking to see if anyone was following. But they did, both of them. Natalie splashed in with a great show of delight, for although she was not a skilled swimmer, she was an enthusiastic one and able to cover some distance. Joshua at last stripped off the T-shirt that had concealed his scarred chest from view, and he, too, followed, striking out strongly into the relatively calm waters of the Sound.

After a while, Christy rolled over in the water and floated, keeping one eye on Natalie's thrashing form closer to shore. What a disturbing afternoon this had been! First Natalie's incisive observations, and then Joshua's arrival on the scene. The passing of weeks without incident, and the telephone conversation with David some time ago, had lulled her into a certain complacency. Not that her physical attraction to Joshua had lessened; if anything, it had grown. But she thought she had hidden it well, and it was distressing to discover that even Natalie had seen evidence of it. She was glad the spelling game had been forgotten long before it had led to skin contact with Joshua. Eye contact was quite bad enough!

A blond head came up beside her in the water, and the reality replaced her turbulent thoughts. Christy thrashed for a moment, then started to tread water.

"You shouldn't surprise people like that!" she scolded Joshua.

"Neither should you," he returned, shaking moisture from his ears. "Why didn't you tell me what Natalie was learning—and what you were learning about her?"

"Because I didn't want to raise false hopes. Frankly, I don't know enough about it to be entirely sure, even yet. But I am certain she's not retarded. Well, except in the sense of being slower to learn. Her IQ must be quite high."

"Come on; we'll swim into shore and talk about it. Natalie will be splashing about for another fifteen minutes at least. Race you in."

And without waiting for an answer, he struck out for the beach with a speed that Christy could not even hope to match. She followed at a deliberately leisurely pace.

By the time she reached shore, Joshua had toweled himself and thrown his large orange beach towel on the sand just in front of the hummocks of poverty grass that led back into higher dunes. The spot was some distance from the water but afforded a clear view of Natalie as she frolicked happily. Joshua was still standing, and with a swift movement at Christy's approach he retrieved his beige T-shirt and was about to pull it over his head.

"Don't do that on my account," Christy said as she neared him. "Please—the scars don't bother me."

He paused with his elbows already in the shirt and gave her a strange look. "They used to. I supposed. . . ." He halted.

"You supposed what?"

"I supposed they still bothered you. You always recoil when I come too close."

Christy's eyes fell away from him, then flew back as she realized she had only given credence to his thoughts. "Your scars have nothing to do with that," she protested.

"Really?" he returned dryly, and pulled the shirt over his head as if he did not believe her. "Now about Natalie," he started, and together they settled on the beach towel. The short distance between them, so often tense, became less so as Christy talked, for this was a topic not fraught with dangers, as others were.

"I'd say she has a perceptual handicap, a severe one. Of course I don't have to explain dyslexia to you; you're a doctor."

"It's not my field. But I did notice the way she wrote her letters backward, and I know that can be due to a perceptual problem."

"Yes. When she printed Natalie and Joshua it was not so obvious; lots of children can get an occasional letter

back-to-front when they're starting. But on 'Brent'—
well, I was thankful you recognized it at all! It's the
same when she tries to read. The letters come out as a
jumble of contradictory messages in her brain. Back to
front, even upside down at times. It's possible she sees
whole words backward. I expect you'll find Natalie has
some motor problems, too; often children like her have
trouble with coordination. Of course, it's all complicated by the fact that she's come to think she's stupid,
and that's the worst thing of all. Children like Natalie
can put up all sorts of defenses against learning once
they come to that conclusion. In her case, the defenses
have been silence and refusal to try things, and the occasional tantrum brought on by frustration. Sometimes
the tantrum appears to be for very little reason at all,
which is why people haven't thought her capable of
learning at her own age level."

"And you think she is?"

"I'm certain of it. She's a bright child, I'm sure. Just
from listening in on classroom work at her schools she
knows how to spell hundreds of simple words, although
she can't read them. You'd have discovered it long ago if
she'd had the kind of individual attention she needs. Or
if she had been properly assessed last spring, as you
planned."

"I take it you're suggesting that should be done at
once."

"Yes. Because you mustn't take my word for any of
this. And then you'll need to send her to a school where
they know the right teaching methods. She needs lots of
help—and confidence. I don't know too much about the
right teaching methods, so I've been working on the
confidence."

"It shows."

"You can thank Natalie for that. She has a streak of

stubbornness in her. She was discouraged but not quite ready to give up altogether. Underneath everything, she really does want to learn. Things will never be easy for her, but I think she'll do well once you get her in the right school."

"Have you told Natalie any of this?"

"No. I think it's best if that comes from the professionals, or from you."

Joshua was silent for a few moments, and with the silence came a returning consciousness of his maleness, his nearness. Finally he spoke, quietly.

"I can't thank you enough, Christy. Of course I'll do what I can, as soon as possible—about the assessment, certainly. But about the school...." He paused, then plunged on recklessly. "I don't like to put her into another boarding school, no matter how good. At least not next year. Would you consider staying with me for a year to tutor Natalie yourself? You have a way with her, and you could read up on the methods. I'd make it well worth your while—pay you double the salary you'd normally earn."

"I couldn't do that," she protested to the beat of a pounding heart.

"Name your own salary, then—your own terms. It's very important to me."

She shook her head without speaking, unable to trust herself to say no. But the fists that tightened against her knees told of the inner turmoil his suggestion had caused.

He went on persuasively, "You told me yourself you weren't getting married for another year. And that school where you were working has gone belly up for lack of funds. Unless you can come up with some excuse that makes sense to me, I won't take no for an answer."

"Please don't press me," she finally said in a strained voice.

"You'll have to do better than that, Christy. Don't you like working with Natalie?"

"That's not it. Please, Dr. Joshua—"

"Joshua. Just plain Joshua. Have you accepted another job?"

"No, but—"

"Then you must agree. Natalie needs you. I need you, too."

"But that's it, don't you see?" Christy burst out. "It's all that needing, and...and I have needs, too. When you're around, I don't trust myself."

Joshua turned slowly until he had her totally in view. Christy's face was in profile, avoiding his, but even from that position she could tell his gaze had fastened on her intently. Feeling that her back was pushed to the wall by his job offer, she had lowered the barriers and made the admission deliberately. And yet some part of her now wanted to disintegrate, to turn into smoke, to vanish before his eyes. He could not possibly have misunderstood her—or could he have?

He had not. "It's not the scars, then, is it." It was phrased like a question, but it was not a question.

"No. That day I told you to stop, it wasn't because of anything I saw. I really did hear Natalie at the door."

He was not quite convinced. "I'm sure I detected a look of horror in your eyes."

"I hardly saw your scars," she said. "And that's not what makes me recoil when you come too close."

"Are you telling me you're actually *attracted*?" He still sounded skeptical.

Christy nodded, still keeping her head averted. "And I have to get over it. I won't if I keep working for you. I told you I trusted my fiancé. But he has to be able to trust me, too, or what kind of marriage is it going to be?

I can't allow myself to turn to putty every time some other man comes within touching distance."

"Some other man?" Joshua asked in a disturbingly low voice.

"You," she admitted simply.

After a moment's silence Joshua spoke again. This time there was a studied offhandedness in his words. "Perhaps you'd better investigate that reaction more fully before you marry." He paused and added idly, "Have you ever had an affair? Other than with your fiancé, I mean."

"No," she said in a muffled voice. "Not even with him."

He looked disbeliving. "Why not?"

Christy stiffened. "That's a very personal question."

"Put it down to the fact that I have a very personal interest."

It mortified her to discuss her inexperience, and so she maintained silence, feeling the crawl of color on her cheeks. Joshua knew only too well that she wasn't immune to caresses, that she didn't have the willpower of a saint. Of course he would be curious about her lack of full response to the man she was supposed to marry.

She felt she couldn't possibly explain to Joshua the flare of annoyance that had been caused by David's methodical approach. During the past few weeks she had done a considerable amount of thinking on the subject, none of it conclusive. But she did recognize one thing: had she been engaged to Joshua, she would have exercised no such restraint. She was aware she would have to deal with those feelings next time she saw David. But this was now, and this was Joshua, and she had to wonder why he was probing in this way....

"You're twenty-four years old," he went on, "and I can testify firsthand that you're anything but frigid.

What have you been doing, living in another universe?"

"If you want to call it that."

"Lack of real attraction to the man or lack of opportunity?"

She was beginning to feel badly trapped. "Does it matter? You can't want to know."

"But I do want to know," he insisted quietly. "Surely you can guess why."

Christy was guessing, although she wasn't sure her guesses were right. Her motives in confessing to her physical attraction for Joshua had not been entirely pure. Her disclosure had been a deliberate encouragement triggered by his job offer but also subconsciously timed to coincide with his discovery that she had a way with his daughter. She knew she would break her engagement to David if Joshua proposed. Her pounding heart told her that was what she hoped for. . . .

Joshua persisted with his questioning. "Could it be you're not really in love with the man? Perhaps you're still trying to make up your mind in some way? That's what it suggests to me."

She forced herself to turn toward him and saw that his gray eyes were intent on her face. She studied him in silence, carefully noting the lean hollow cheeks, the hard line of his mouth and jaw. His expression was sensuous and ascetic all at once. By now Christy recognized it as a look of tamped-down sexuality, an expression he often wore, especially when alone with her. "Perhaps," she said guardedly.

"Then I suggest you'd better have a proper affair with me." His voice remained impersonal, almost aloof, as if his emotions were in no way involved. She stared at him, her heart sinking, wishing she had not confessed her weakness for his physical attractions. Her secrecy had provided armor of a kind during the past weeks. Now the armor was gone, and he wanted no more from her than he had ever wanted.

"Have an affair with me," he went on, relentlessly and dispassionately. Christy listened numbly, unable to stop him. "An affair—then you'll be sure before you marry. You can't tie yourself to this fellow—David—if there's a chance it's the wrong thing to do. Good God, if he hasn't taken you by storm in all these years there must be something wrong! He's either untrustworthy or undersexed. Do you really want a lifetime of being sexually mismatched?" Despite his hands clenching and unclenching at the edges of the beach towel, his voice remained matter-of-fact, as if he were discussing the weather. "You'd better find out, hadn't you? Marriage is much too important to leave to chance."

Christy ran a tongue over lips that felt excruciatingly dry, but the salty surface of them only put a bad taste in her mouth. She turned her head away and stared at Natalie, who was now collecting shells and stones by the water's edge. At this moment she hated this tall gaunt blond man beside her—hated him for what he was suggesting in such an unfeeling manner, hated him for having such power over her that she was listening. How could he be so detached? Where was the passion she remembered?

He went on, displaying none of it. "I suggest you have an affair with me. I said I wouldn't have an affair with Natalie in the next room, and I won't. But I can make arrangements. Mrs. Cousins can mind Natalie for—"

"Stop it!" Christy held her hands to her ears. "I can't listen anymore. If I wanted to have an affair I'd have had one long ago—with David. He's not undersexed, as you put it. He's tried often enough, and at least he has the grace to suggest it when he's saying good-night—not

like this. And with marriage as a part of the bargain . . .
not just a job."

Joshua's silence became unnerving. Finally he said
slowly, "Would marriage make a difference?"

Her own answer was almost as long in coming, and it
was barely whispered into her knees. "It might." It
would, but pride prevented her from saying so. He had
still offered nothing, only broached the subject.

"I suppose it occurs to you that I might make the offer
because of Natalie."

Christy made no answer to that, so the next words
came from Joshua again, astonishing her with their
sudden ferocity. "Well, I won't. I got married once
because of Natalie. I won't do it again." He slammed a
fist against the sand, angrily, and his voice became
cruel, deliberately hurtful. "Oh, yes, Christy, Natalie
was on the way when I married her mother. Don't look
so shocked! Not everybody has the forbearance of your
fiancé."

She shook her head, still stunned by the vehemence of
his response. "I wasn't shocked in that way," she
denied, with impulses to cry burning at her eyelids. "It
was just the outburst. It was so sudden. After you had
been so . . . so cold-blooded before."

"Cold-blooded?" He gave a short strangled laugh. "If
there's one thing I'm not, it's cold-blooded. Oh,
Christy . . . ." His hand stretched toward her; straining
fingertips touched her hair, her temples, her eyelids.
"Can't you see I'm frustrated—wanting you and half out
of my mind with it? Don't you see I can't trust myself to
approach you any other way, after what happened the
last time? I couldn't offer you an affair casually, along
with a good-night kiss. I wouldn't be willing to stop
with the kiss, no matter what you said. Oh, God . . . ."

His fingertips held anguish, passion, promise. To

Christy their touch was unbearable. She wrenched herself away and turned her back to him. Behind her he moved swiftly. His legs trapped her, one on each side, the long muscled stretch of them darkly bronzed against the silver sand. His sun-heated body was close against her spine, and his arms came around her waist, fiercely possessive. His hands stroked her bared flesh, moving in urgent arousing patterns over her stomach. And then his progress took him downward. He insinuated his thumb just beneath the edge of bikini at her hip and ran it in a tantalizing path along the verge of cloth, skirting more intimate discoveries. She sucked in her breath, closed her eyes, and arched her head against his shoulder.

"I want you," he said fiercely. "You, you, you...I want you so damn much I toss most of every night. I'm obsessed with you and you know it. How can you call me cold-blooded? You know bloody well I'm not!"

Christy's moment of weakness was short. "Joshua," she began in a sudden panic. "Natalie...for heaven's sake, think of Natalie."

He released her and moved backward by a few inches. His legs still bracketed her effectively enough, his knees and virile calves now enclosing her hips. His feet dug into the sand beside her upper thighs.

He laughed, a short harsh laugh. "Believe me, I'm more aware of the dangers than you are. I don't think my daughter's quite ready for a lesson in male anatomy. But...oh, God if she weren't within a stone's throw I'd show you what you do to my blood."

Suddenly his hands were warm on her shoulder blades, moving in slow seductive circles that caused her skin to quiver. His voice became low, vibrant, convincing, caressing her emotions as surely as his fingers caressed her spine. She closed her eyes, but the sun seemed to penetrate her lids, inescapable and pervasive, as were the wanton wonderful inducements he offered with his words.

"Come somewhere with me tomorrow night," he murmured. "We don't have to go far. The Graydunes beach is very, very private. I'll be careful with you, darling. I'll teach you to make love as you should be taught...no ifs and buts, and nothing held back. God, if you knew how much I've needed a woman like you! A warm, willing, giving woman...."

All at once his voice fell silent and his hand grew still. It was not snatched away from her spine—he left it resting lightly against the flesh—but Christy knew what had happened. Schooling her expression to clothe the ruinous emotions inside, she raised her head in time to see Natalie's approach.

"Oh, dad!" Natalie squealed with pleasure. She ran the last few steps and dropped to a sitting position beside her father. "You're playing my game."

"That we are," replied Joshua slowly. Other than an unusual timbre his voice bore no traces of the suppressed passion it had held only moments earlier. "But Christy plays it much better with you. I don't think she understands me at all."

I understand you, thought Christy, *and marriage was not a part of the deal.* But she could not say it; nor could she continue to sit like this, with her back turned and Joshua's hand resting lightly on her spine. With a supreme effort of will she turned to face father and daughter, her smile forced.

"Hi, Natalie," she managed rather shakily.

"You're teasing dad." Natalie's pansy eyes were mischievous. "You know what he was spelling. You always do."

Christy shook her head. "No. I...." But she could

say no more, and looked to Joshua with an unspoken plea for help.

His darkened eyes spoke solemn messages across the air between them. "Perhaps Christy wasn't listening to my hands, Natalie," he said unsmilingly. "It was a very simple word I spelled. Yes. That's what I want to hear her say. Yes."

"No," said Christy, and Natalie shrieked with laughter.

7

THE NEXT DAY was a Tuesday, and there were three important phone calls. The first was made by Joshua, long-distance to New York, but Christy did not find out about that until later. Today was a day to avoid him like the plague, and for the most part she succeeded.

The second phone call came from David, just past noon. Mrs. Cousins called Christy from the sunroom, where she had been teaching Natalie some basic facts about weather: an appropriate topic for a day when the weeping skies shaped everyone's doings. It was raining steadily, one of those slow summer rains that wash the whole world with pale pastel colors. A good day to stay inside.

There were several extensions for the telephone—one in Joshua's bedroom, one in the kitchen, one in the library—and it was in this last room that Christy took the call. It was a room she loved. The wing chairs were not antiques, but they were old all the same, and shabbier than the furniture elsewhere in the house. An ancient rolltop desk sat in one corner. The crammed bookshelves held the collection of several generations, a fascinating miscellany that covered everything from whaling to quilting, from Kafka to Conrad, from Hemingway to Hans Christian Andersen. Between the books, jammed into every available nook and cranny of shelf space, were fine pieces of scrimshaw—whalebone depicting scenes scratched by long-forgotten sailors in their leisure hours at sea. A brick fireplace promised long cozy winter nights, but at the moment it remained unlit.

There was an oversized leather-covered couch near the phone, and Christy settled herself on it before she picked up the receiver.

"Hello. . .David?"

There was a click of the kitchen receiver being cradled back into place as Mrs. Cousins hung up.

"Christy, what took you so long? These minutes cost, you know. I thought you'd be at lunch."

"I'm sorry, David—this is a wonderful surprise! Oh, you don't know how I've needed to talk to you. I tried to call you late last night when I knew you'd be off duty, but they couldn't find—"

He cut through her words. "Got to make this short, Christy. This phone call's not in the budget, remember! There's good news. I have a chance to come to Nantucket for a few days."

Why the sinking feeling in her stomach, when she had felt such a need to see him?

"Christy, did you hear me?"

"Yes. . .yes, of course. How wonderful! But that's not in the budget, either, is it? I mean, how—"

"Private plane. I'm hitching a ride with a friend of mine. I have four days coming to me, and it happens he's going to Nantucket over the weekend. Friday till Monday night, if I can get the time."

"What luck, David. It will be awfully good to—"

"The plans are all worked out," he broke in, "except for one hitch. I can't afford a hotel. Do you think I can put up there? You said it was a huge house."

"I don't know. I'll have to ask."

"Tell old what's-his-face—Dr. Brent—that it's in a good cause. Fellow medical practitioner and all that.

He's bound to allow it. Find out and call me back tonight, for sure. Tomorrow morning I have to put in a request for the time."

"I think you can plan on it, David, no matter what he says. You can stay in a hotel if need be. In fact I'll make a reservation for you. I—it's important to me to have you come."

"Why—something wrong? You sound upset."

"No, nothing. It's just that— Oh, David, perhaps we should have been married last spring. The waiting has done something to me—I can't explain on the telephone. I'll tell you when I see you."

There was a second sharp silence on the line, then David's voice again. "Are you trying to tell me you're finally ready to do...what I want you to do?"

"Oh, *David*—"

"Well, are you? All it takes is a little forethought."

"David, please don't talk like that."

There was a swearword on the other end, one Christy did not particularly like to hear. "This time I won't take no for an answer. Good Lord, we've been engaged for three years, Christy! In another year we'll be married. Make the arrangements!"

Again there was a moment's silence, broken by David. "Christy—Christy, are you still there? Look, this is costing. Call me back tonight—anytime after midnight. I'll wait by the phone."

"All right," she agreed despondently.

"I love you, honey. And remember."

"I love you, too, David," she replied, but the words came out of habit, not conviction. And then he rang off; and through the lunch that followed Christy found herself with very little appetite at all.

Things were very wrong with her engagement, and she could not even blame David, much as she would have liked to. David had not changed; she had. Had she ever truly loved him, or had he always just been a form of self-defense? A defense against the kind of involvement Joshua Brent wanted from her? David wanted that kind of involvement, too—but his overtures were predictable and manageable, and always had been. During her weeks of wondering, she had often enumerated David's good qualities. There was a warmth and security in being with him. David was dependable, determined, positive in a way that had always allowed Christy to feel feminine in his presence. He had never wanted to be babied, and she needed that in a man—a mastery, a masculinity, a self-assurance, a strength. David had strengths. Strengths that would someday mean a happy marriage . . . a kind of loving that she knew would grow.

She had always wanted to marry. A husband, a home, children—these had always seemed important to Christy. Love had been a fundamental part of the warm home in which she'd been reared. But love had seemed a giving, living, sharing, growing thing. Like a plant, it thrived if given the right proportions of shade and sunshine, nourishment and attention; and even, at times, a little healthy neglect. She still believed this, rationally, even now, and she had always known she could find this satisfying kind of marriage with David if she worked hard at it. With time and patience, theirs would be a lasting relationship.

And what did Joshua offer as an alternative? Something wild, wondrous, passionate, unprincipled—and almost unbearably tempting. He asked her to give everything, to hold back nothing. And she wanted to; how she wanted to! Yet what was he willing to give her, beyond his own need? Love should be more than a blaze of temporary passion; more than a fire that consumed the vitals and fed on the soul and then, at last, left the emotions a scorched ruin. Any temporary liaison with Dr. Joshua Brent would destroy her; she knew that. Destroy any chance of the other, lasting kind of love. And yet, and yet, and yet . . . .

"Christy, child, you've hardly eaten a bite!"

Christy pulled herself out of her painful reverie to Mrs. Cousins's worried words. She put a smile on her face, but it was less than successful. "I'm not hungry today. I guess it's the rain—not enough exercise."

"Exercise! You were a hundred miles away in your head, and you looked as though you'd walked every inch of the way. That's the third time I've spoken to you, Christy. And minutes ago you put six lumps of sugar into your coffee, and you never take more than two."

"I did not!" Christy replied, managing a shaky laugh. "I couldn't drink it with six. And as you see, it's all gone."

"You did, too," claimed Natalie, supporting Mrs. Cousins. "I counted, and we laughed about it, Mrs. Cousins and me. You didn't even hear us."

"Mrs. Cousins and I," corrected Christy automatically in an abstracted voice.

"Not something to do with that phone call, was it?" asked the housekeeper solicitously. "Not that I like to pry."

"Of course not," returned Christy, making great efforts to overcome the depression that threatened to swamp her. "It was good news. My fiancé is coming to Nantucket next weekend. I was dreaming about it, that's all."

Mrs. Cousins's eyes narrowed suspiciously. "Dreaming with that glum look on your face? I must say, I'd hate to see you after some *really* good news."

Christy knew her behavior could not pass without

some explanation; and since she could not tell the truth, she prevaricated. "Well, actually I was worried about...about the cost of it all. We're saving our money for a house, you see, and David can't really afford trips like that. It's quite an expense. He may decide not to come. I promised I'd phone him tonight."

"Well, certainly he should be able to stay here and save that part of the money! Lands sakes, what's one more to cook for? Already I'm giving Tom Maybee most of his meals now, and six is just as easy as five. Easier! Recipes never work out for five people." Mrs. Cousins stood up and went to the sink, bearing her plate and Natalie's.

"Dr. Joshua would never agree," demurred Christy. "And I wouldn't want to ask him. No—it's best if David stays in a hotel."

"You couldn't get a reservation now," observed Mrs. Cousins in a pleasant tone. "And why wouldn't Dr. Joshua agree? Of course he would!"

"I'll ask for you," Natalie piped up. "Dad won't say no to me."

"You will not ask your dad," said Christy spiritedly.

"Will not ask what?" came a voice from the doorway, and Joshua stepped into the kitchen, returning his luncheon tray from the second floor.

"If Christy's fiancé can stay here for a few days," Natalie informed him at once.

Joshua grew silent for a few moments, and beneath his measuring gaze Christy's eyes fell. Finally he said, in a decidedly unfriendly voice, "When is he coming—and for how long?"

"Just for the weekend," mumbled Christy to her half-eaten omelet. "Friday till Monday night."

Joshua put the tray down noisily. "Perhaps it would be best if he stayed in a hotel," he said with unmistakable hostility.

"Oh, dad!" Natalie stared at her father in dismay and disbelief. "You don't mean that! Christy hasn't seen him for months!"

"Miss Christy's fiancé hasn't enough money to stay elsewhere." Mrs. Cousins, turning from the sink to face Joshua, added her persuasions to Natalie's. There was a tight-lipped look about her mouth, as though she could not quite believe what her ears had just told her. "If he can't stay here, he may not be able to come at all. And it's no trouble for meals, Dr. Brent," she added, with a formality in her term of address that she did not customarily use.

"That's right, dad. You can't say no! Christy looked so *lonely* for him. She has to phone him tonight, and he won't come if he can't stay here."

Joshua looked from one to the other; then at Christy, whose head remained bowed, curtaining her expression. "All right, then," he said in a tight voice. "It's agreed." And he strode out of the room without another word.

"Well, can you figure that!" exclaimed Mrs. Cousins with her hands on her hips, staring at the empty doorway through which his tall rangy frame had just vanished. But in Natalie's presence she said no more.

"Oh, I expect he doesn't want the household routine upset in any way," said Christy as lightly as possible, in an effort to pour oil on troubled waters. "After all, he's still trying to regain his strength. Perhaps he's worried that David and I will be noisy or inconsiderate. Or that Natalie's lessons will suffer."

"Well, he can't know you very well," observed Mrs. Cousins, going back to her work and clattering dishes into the sink with more force than was strictly necessary.

"Perhaps I'll try the hotels anyway," said Christy uncomfortably, and later that afternoon she did. But

Mrs. Cousins had been right: all accommodations for the weekend had long since been booked. David would have to stay at Graydunes or not at all. So Christy gave in to the idea. She had not lied to David about needing to see him. But the problem remained: what did she intend to say to him when she did see him?

The third important phone call of the day took place, strictly speaking, at the very beginning of the following day, for it was after midnight when Christy made good her promise to David. She had not seen Joshua since noon. Recently, with returning health, he had grown accustomed to eating the evening meal in the dining room with Christy and Natalie, but tonight he had chosen to dine in his own room, and Christy sensed it had something to do with what had happened earlier in the day. Yet surely he could not in all conscience be jealous of David! David, who had a prior claim on her affections; David, who at least cared enough for her to offer marriage.

Bedtime at Graydunes came early for everyone. Christy had bathed and prepared herself for the night at ten o'clock, as was her custom. Now, with midnight showing on her watch, she slipped a loose Japanese silk kimono—a gift from a seafaring uncle—over her shorty nightgown and started down the hall on soundless bare feet. A glimpse down both corridors told her that all others in the household had settled for the night. Without the skylight flooding her vision, it was easy enough to see whether there were slivers of light beneath the doors—and there were none, she noted. Not even under Joshua's door. Especially Joshua's door. Christy had been prepared to turn back and dress more adequately if there were signs of wakefulness in his room.

There was a dim bulb burning in the lower hall, enough to light her passage. She made her way to the library and, groping in the dark, found the switch for an ancient lamp with a mottled mica shade. It cast very little light, but it was enough for her purposes. Pulling the kimono close around her, for it had no sash, she settled on the couch and dialed.

David must have been waiting by the phone he shared with several other interns, for he answered at once.

"Well? What's the verdict?" he asked as soon as the greetings were dispensed with.

"You can stay at Graydunes," Christy informed him. "But I may not be able to see as much of you as you'd like. I have to mind Natalie. The little girl."

"Oh, I'll help with her," David said agreeably enough. "I like kids. You know that." It was true—and one of the things that had endeared him to Christy so many years ago. "Anyway, you don't have to mind her all the time. Didn't you tell me lessons were over by four-thirty?"

But of course, remembered Christy—she had never told him of the change in arrangement so many weeks before. "I forgot to tell you, David. There's no nanny now. I look after Natalie all the time."

"Oh, *hell*! When did that happen?"

"Weeks ago. But she's no trouble—really she isn't. Her father takes her part of the time, too. And it won't stop us from going out in the evening. Mrs. Cousins can always take over at bedtime."

"I hope Old Sourpuss is paying you the nanny's wages, too," said David in a disgruntled tone.

"Well, no," admitted Christy. "I didn't ask for more money, and Dr. Brent probably forgot to suggest it. He's paying me very well as it is. And really, David, he isn't exactly an old...."

A small noise attracted her attention to the doorway, and she glanced upward. Shock robbed her muscles of strength temporarily, and the phone clattered noisily to the floor.

Joshua was standing in the doorway. He was still fully dressed, in black trousers and a black cotton turtleneck. The dark clothes made his body seem almost just another shadow and drew startling attention to his chiseled ascetic face and the silvery gold fairness of his hair.

Christy sprang to her feet, pulses pounding—then remembered David and the telephone. With her eyes still on that unnerving tall apparition in the doorway, she bent down and retrieved the receiver, holding her kimono close about her waist.

"Christy—Christy, are you there? Are you all right?" the voice was coming from the other end.

"Yes, I . . . I'm all right," she said faintly.

"What happened?"

"I . . . dropped the receiver, that's all."

"Did something give you a shock? You sound dazed."

"No, it's just clumsiness. Nothing happened."

"Oh. What were you saying about Dr. Brent?"

"I don't remember." He was coming across the room now. Closer, closer . . . the pool of lamplight caught his hair, gilding it for the moment, and then he had walked past, into the shadowed spaces near Christy. Closer. Achingly close. . . .

"I think you were about to say he wasn't an old sourpuss. So you're starting to like him a little better. But not too much, I hope?"

"No—yes—that is . . . ." Christy felt faint, unable to concentrate on the conversation. Joshua had moved so close she could feel his breath fanning her cheek. And she could not move away. She was already backed into a corner formed by the couch and the table where the telephone stood.

"What *is* the matter, Christy? Is someone there with you?"

She shook her head, then realized David could not hear such a gesture over the phone. "No," she said in a weak voice. "I'm...quite alone. But I'm not feeling too well. I want to hang up."

"Don't hang up, for heaven's sake. I have to give you some more information about arrival times and that sort of thing. You're not feeling *that* sick, are you? It's a bit sudden."

Joshua's eyes had turned decidedly derisive at her lie. They glinted dangerously as he closed in by a few more vital inches. He stood so near she could feel the warmth of his body, could distinguish the grainy texture of his skin and the tiny mocking lines at the corners of his eyes. She could detect the throb of a pulse in his strong throat and the almost invisible blond stubble of a jaw unshaven since early morning. And she could not even push him away, for to do so would be to lose her grip on the kimono front and risk exposure.

She struggled to control herself. "No—no. I'll be all right. I was just a little dizzy." With the male aura of Joshua swirling into her nostrils, that much was true, but it was a lame excuse. Christy added, "Actually, David, I've been under the weather all day with a touch of flu."

Her second lie caused Joshua's mouth to turn scornful. He lifted one hand and tugged gently at her nose, as if to extend it in Pinocchio fashion. The brief gesture ended as soon as Christy made an evasive move, but its meaning was clear.

"Oh? Well, it can't be too bad or you'd have mentioned it earlier," crackled the receiver. "Well, now, let's see...we were talking about my plans. Lenny's flying me there Friday, probably around suppertime. I'll be staying until Monday or Tuesday, I'm not sure which. D'you think Dr. Brent would send that Jeep of his to pick me up at the airport? Or has old sourpuss loosened up that much?"

Joshua must have been able to hear what David said. His brows shot up quizzically and his mouth formed an ironic O. He bent and blew gently at Christy's ear, stirring the hair near the lobe.

Her dizziness turned to acute vertigo. "No, he hasn't," she said with difficulty, causing a cynical gleam to enter Joshua's eye.

Joshua moved his attentions to her mouth, blowing a taunting trail across her cheek until the tang of his warm breath mingled with her own. Her head reeling, Christy could think of no way to stop him. "Besides, David," she said with effort, "I think it's a...a bit much to ask."

In desperation she considered sitting down on the couch to put some distance between her and her tormentor but immediately thought better of it. With Joshua around it seemed safer to be vertical. On a couch it would be too easy to end up totally horizontal and totally vulnerable.

"Well, look, if no one can meet me, I'll take a taxi. I guess the budget can stretch to that. But I'll phone you from the airport, just in case. So ask, will you? Old sourpuss might surprise you. From what you say he wasn't too put out when you wanted to have me there for the weekend."

The sardonic twist of Joshua's mouth told her he had heard that small exchange, too, and intended to make her pay for her various prevarications. He lifted one hand and dragged a tantalizing fingertip over her lips. He probed lightly, then trailed the moisture of her mouth over one cheek, making a slow featherlight passage toward the ear not covered by the telephone. With exquisitely seductive movements his fingers started to stroke the exposed lobe.

Christy let out a soft involuntary gasp. "Oh!"

"What's that? What's going on, Christy?"

"Nothing! Absolutely nothing."

But it was not nothing. Her new lie merely darkened the derisive gleam in Joshua's eyes. In payment his fingers continued to do deliberately erotic things to her ear. With the curve of his sensuous lips mesmerizing her, she couldn't think of what to say next.

David's voice became businesslike again. "There's no need to have a bed made up for me. Provided you've started on the pill, I intend to move right into yours. Okay?"

Joshua's brows flew skyward and his mouth became absolutely intransigent. His fingers moved into Christy's hair and tightened to the point of pain. Angrily he formed the soundless word "no."

Christy opened her mouth to speak, and immediately Joshua leaned forward to dip into the opening, rubbing the tip of his tongue briefly against hers. He backed off almost at once, allowing her the freedom to talk, but with his male taste in her mouth she could no longer think of what she had been going to say. Joshua was looking at her sternly, and that didn't help her thought processes. His fingers remained in her hair, their hold less fierce but no less disruptive than earlier.

The silence on the other end of the phone reminded her that David was waiting for some kind of response. Her spiraling senses prevented her from remembering what they had been discussing. With a supreme effort she remembered he had said something about taking a taxi from the airport. "That's a...a good idea, David," she said weakly.

Again Joshua's mouth formed an angry "no," and she

remembered they hadn't been talking about taxis at all. They had been talking about beds.

"On second thought, Dr. Brent wouldn't approve," she added, her head swimming.

Joshua nodded grimly, pleased with at least one of her answers. His grip on her hair eased, and he began to massage her scalp with his fingertips. Unutterably stirred by the disturbing feel of his moving hand in her hair, Christy had to stifle a low moan. She felt incapable of movement.

"Oh, hell. Then he really is a disagreeable sort, isn't he? I hoped we could be aboveboard. I hate doing things on the sly."

"So...so do I," Christy said, her voice uneven.

Joshua's lids drooped dangerously, for she hadn't told David what was happening on the sly right at this very moment. His free hand came around her—not to hold but to inflict a new punishment. His fingernail dragging down her spine caused erotic and excruciating shivers.

"Stop," Christy begged breathlessly, shuddering and arching to escape the torture.

"Stop what?" David asked.

She cast about desperately. "Stop...stop talking that way about...about Dr. Brent."

"Honestly, Christy, sometimes I don't understand you. You're the one who told me he was a bad-tempered bastard."

Hearing the description, Joshua smiled grimly and nodded in mocking acknowledgment. At once both his hands started a slow, supremely agonizing journey toward her breasts. It was clear he intended some new vengeance. There was a small cruel curl to his lips as his two thumbs insinuated themselves under the edge of her kimono, parting it where it covered her breasts. Soon his fingers were on her nipples, gently rolling them.

Now there was no point in clutching at the waist of the kimono, so Christy let go of the fabric bunched in her hand and started to push at his chest. It was a feeble effort, and Joshua didn't move away. Where her hand connected with the hard wall of him, the feel of his muscled warmth beneath the thin turtleneck was yet another stimulant to her touch.

"David, I can't...."

"Can't what?"

"Think," she groaned. "I can't think. I'm feeling absolutely wretched."

The first part was true, but the second part wasn't, and Joshua knew it. He was already aware of the springing response beneath his fingers, the budding evidence of her desire. Hearing her most recent untruth, he merely applied firmer pressure to her nipples, staking his claim until the delicious squeezing became a sweet and terrible torment.

"Christy, are you sure there's nobody there with you? I hear some pretty hard breathing."

"There's...nobody," Christy said faintly, then sucked in her breath sharply as Joshua's hands shot down to clamp her waist beneath the kimono. In the same swift instant he bent his head and bit a nipple through the thin lawn of her nightgown. The sharp nip was a punishment for her new fabrication, but she couldn't take it back without explaining everything to David, and her brain was whirling far too much to allow explanations of any kind.

"What was that?" David asked suspiciously.

"I...I broke a fingernail," Christy fibbed, earning herself another excruciating tightening of teeth. Pushing ineffectually at Joshua's head, she tried to resume the interrupted conversation, talking hurriedly now in order to end it as soon as possible. "Let me know if you get the time off. Phone me tomorrow with the rest of the details. David, I *must* go."

"Wait! Don't hang up. I don't want to have to call you tomorrow. For God's sake, Christy, use a little reason! Think of the daytime rates."

Joshua's tongue had become an acute torture. With the crest of her breast still trapped firmly between his teeth, he bathed the sensitive tip. And when he moved onward to assault a second target, she could see the darkness of her own taut flesh gleaming provocatively through the wet clinging patch of fabric.

Christy thought she was going to swoon. The wild fluttering of her pulses and the racing heat of her blood were causing unutterable reactions to waken in every secret inch of skin, and she could think of no way to escape. At this point she would have gladly broken the contact by collapsing onto the couch, but Joshua's fingers digging into her waist prevented it. He had also propped a foot against the edge of the couch, so that she couldn't possibly sidle past him. She was trapped—and not only by her own lies.

"If your flu is really that bad, why don't you get some medicine from Dr. Brent?" David grumbled. "I don't want you in bed for the whole weekend—only part of it."

"Yes. . .I mean no. . .I mean. . . ."

"What *do* you mean?"

"I mean yes. . .I will. . .get some. . .some medicine," she agonized, as the feel of the rubbing tongue at her breast inundated her with giant waves of longing.

"I think you ought to get hold of something tonight," David said slowly, worried at last. "I don't like the way you're sounding. Better go and see Dr. Brent as soon as you get off the phone. Promise?"

"I. . .couldn't do. . .that," she managed brokenly.

"Why not? He's right there. It's not as though he has to make a house call. Now promise you'll go and get something from him—tonight."

"I...couldn't...wake him," Christy whispered, in total anguish. "He...he's...an invalid."

Joshua glanced upward with his mouth still fastened on a captive nipple, and the look in his eye told her that thanks to this last piece of deception she was about to get some very strong medicine indeed. Immediately he turned his attentions to the lower half of her body.

David was talking and she could hardly hear a word he was saying. None of it seemed to make sense. The whole world was whirling. One of Joshua's arms had come around beneath her kimono and his hand was pressed closely against her buttock, capturing it. His splayed fingers caressed it seductively through the thin nightie, even as his other hand touched her thighs.

She clamped her legs tightly against him, but his fingers were still there, moving with intimate insistence. Christy closed her eyes and bit her lips to prevent a moan from escaping. The weeks of severe frustration, fed by frequent erotic dreams all of which involved Joshua, had left her in a state of quivering readiness. She felt on the point of some volcanic catastrophe. But she didn't want Joshua to know that, and so she forced herself to remain still, pushing ineffectually at his hand, locking her legs to prevent the wild tremble of her knees.

She became dimly aware that David was waiting for some kind of response. She tried to think what it might be. Strange shudders of longing were sweeping through her, chasing one another along her legs and through her thighs and up past the tingling pit of her stomach.

Joshua withdrew his hands, and that gave her some brief relief. Her passion-glazed eyes came open, and she

saw that her disobedient fingers had somehow become
tightly laced into his hair. With an effort she released
her grip. He straightened at once, and it appeared that
he was about to move away. From the heaviness of his
eyes and the severe tenseness in his face she could see he
had become mightily aroused.

She couldn't imagine what David was waiting
to hear. "I have to...go now," she whispered ragged-
ly.

"Christy, for God's sake pull yourself together!"
David was sounding distinctly irritable. "I know you
have to go. Didn't I just say good-night? But don't you
have anything else to say to me?"

"No, I—"

"What do you usually say when you say good-night
to your fiancé? Surely you can manage that much."

"I...love you," she obliged faintly. But she wasn't
sure who she was saying it to. Her drugged eyes were on
Joshua's lean face. Hearing her, his mouth curled with
sardonic contempt. He knew she had told another lie.

"Now go and get some rest," David finished. "I want
that flu over with before I get there. See you Friday,
honey."

Christy's fingers were practically tying knots in the
telephone cord. Joshua's hands were reaching for her
again. He intended to make her pay for her final pre-
varication.

"Good-night," she managed. The receiver clattered
back onto its rest, and she fell against the sofa, twisting
violently, tearing at his hair, trying to evade a renewal
of intimate caresses. But in the next second his hard
hands captured her....

An explosion of sensation greeted the moment when
his fingers made contact. Shooting stars skyrocketed
through her veins; fireworks exploded; volcanoes

erupted. And then the whole world dissolved into a lava flow of molten gold.

When she recovered from the exquisite shuddering, she realized she was alone on the couch. Joshua was no longer holding her. He had retreated by several feet to take refuge in a nearby chair and nurse a difficult dose of frustration. His eyes were closed, his head thrown back, his face pained.

Christy sat up and straightened herself. She pulled her kimono close about her, trembling in the aftermath of her shattering experience. She took several silent minutes to recover. When she felt herself capable of speech, she glared at Joshua from across the relative safety of space. "How could you—how *could* you!"

Joshua's eyes came slowly open. The embers of difficult desire still glowed and flickered in their depths. For him there had been no culmination, no moment of release to end the arousing contact. "Forgive me," he apologized in a strained unnatural voice. "I'd be over there now but for one thing. Natalie wakened when she heard me coming downstairs. I don't expect her to come down, but—"

"You know that's not what I mean!" Christy lifted her chin in a quivering challenge. "How *dare* you do those things while I'm talking to my fiancé on the phone?"

Joshua straightened in his chair. With partial control restored, his eyes turned taunting. "Why did you lie to him? You had no reason to tell him you were alone. If I hadn't heard that particular piece of deceit, I wouldn't have dreamed of taking advantage. And then when you kept on telling untruths...."

"That's no excuse!"

"Maybe not. But the temptation was too trying. I knew you could hardly stop me, short of hanging up or admitting your little fib. Dammit, Christy, it's your own fault. If you weave a tangled web you're bound to get caught in it. And you have the presumption to talk about trust!"

"Isn't there a little presumption on your part, too? You broke a promise—a promise not to touch me."

"You released me yesterday. And now that I know why you wanted the promise, that it wasn't just my scars—"

"That was *yesterday*," she broke in. "I haven't released you forever. Things haven't changed." Then, when he made a move to rise from his chair, she said in a low tight voice, "Stay away, Joshua, or you have my resignation. Effective at once."

"Christy—"

"I mean it. I won't have an affair." She made a helpless gesture with her one free hand. "I don't believe in the kind of love you're offering—here today, gone tomorrow. Passion without promises...I don't want it, Joshua. I happen to think the other kinds of love are more important in the long run."

Joshua stood up and started to pace the floor. "And in the long run, do you think you'll get them from that, that— *Hell*, Christy, I could hear his voice on the phone. He sounded like a computer bank. You can't seriously want to marry him."

"I'm not sure about anything anymore. Except one thing. With you, Joshua," she said, and there was a tremor in her voice, "there is no long run."

"Oh, God, Christy." Across the room she could see his whitened knuckles, the lines of tautness around his mouth. "Don't try to push me into anything."

"Push you...?" She shook her head in slow denial. "I'm not trying to push you into anything. How can you think it? If marriage isn't in your plans, that's your business. But it happens to be in mine, and I won't be pushed into an affair. Now if you don't mind...."

But before she could gather herself together to go, he strode swiftly across the room and came to a halt not three feet away, between Christy and the door, barring her exit. "Wait, Christy. You can't go now—not until you've heard what I came downstairs to tell you. Sit down. I won't touch you again. But, dammit, I've been waiting all night for you to make that phone call, so I could catch you alone in fairly neutral territory. You see—" he gave a short bitter laugh "—I wasn't totally without principles. I didn't try to come to your bedroom."

"How did you know I would be using the phone—" she started; then remembered that Natalie had mentioned that fact, in Joshua's presence, earlier in the day. All the same, how had he known to find her downstairs at this particular time? She made no sound coming down the stairs, she was sure.

"The phone in my bedroom has a peculiar habit of making a little jingling sound whenever one of the other receivers is picked up. Frankly, I've been lying down in the dark waiting for it, and for the first time in weeks I didn't curse the telephone company when it happened."

"Oh." She looked down at her bare feet, unsure of what to do next. What could Joshua possibly say that he had not already said? Was he going to tell her that David could not stay here after all? She looked up. "If it's about David coming—"

"No, it's not." His jaw tightened momentarily. "I agreed he could stay here, and although I don't much like the idea, I won't back out now—although I intend to keep a damn close eye on what goes on while he's around. It's about some other matters. First, Natalie. Why don't you sit down? This is going to take a while."

Christy opened her mouth to object and then thought better of it. If it was about Natalie, she could hardly refuse to listen. And she ought to be adult enough to stay, because embarrassment wasn't enough of a reason for running. If the encounter by the telephone had done nothing else, it had given her some temporary immunity to Joshua's attractions. She wouldn't melt like warm butter now; and anyway, if Joshua intended to take advantage, he could have done so with a great deal more ease a short time earlier.

Putting her feelings on ice, she moved back toward the couch and perched on its overstuffed arm, ready for flight if necessary.

As for Joshua, he remained standing, or rather walking. There was tension in every line of his lean-limbed body; a tension he worked out by moving around the floor restlessly, as though he found it unbearable to remain long in one place.

"About Natalie. I made a phone call first thing this morning—to the place that was to have done that assessment last January. A small hospital. Its director happens to be a doctor I knew in medical school, and to tell the truth, I've been pulling a few strings. I explained your theories—what you thought about her problems, how important it might be to get her into the right kind of school at once. Assuming, of course, you refuse to take the job I offered." He looked at Christy for a penetrating moment and saw that she had not changed her mind. "He agrees with you that something should be done. He's promised to move heaven and earth to take her in for the assessment as soon as possible. By tomorrow I should hear something."

"That's wonderful," Christy interposed.

Again he gave her a peculiar look, a look Christy found quite piercing and disturbing. His voice remained impersonal, however. "It will mean a trip to New York, of course. The assessment will take the better part of a week. She'll be admitted overnight several times, for various tests: electroencephalograms, blood-sugar tests, that sort of thing, just to make sure there's nothing physical involved. But she'll be an outpatient most of the time—in by nine, out by five. I'll explain to Natalie as soon as I've been given an admission date."

Christy nodded. "I think you've done the right thing."

"Good." He swung around on his heel and walked farther away, toward the bookshelves. He remained silent for a few moments, frowning; then he picked up a piece of scrimshaw and directed his attention to it when he spoke again. "We'll fly to New York. There's no point in driving, and in Manhattan it's best to take taxis anyway, or walk. My penthouse is quite centrally located. I don't think you'll need to take a large number of clothes—"

"What is this?" Christy was on her feet, face pale beneath the summer's tan. "An offer I can't refuse?"

Joshua's eyes glittered. "I don't see how you can refuse, as it's part of your job. I'll need help with Natalie."

"Is Mrs. Cousins coming?"

"I see no need for her. We'll eat most of our main meals in restaurants. That will make it fun for Natalie—an adventure."

"And what kind of adventure do you have in mind for the nights she's in hospital?" Christy found her body trembling all over, her teeth near chattering. She willed herself to calm down, without success.

"That's up to you," Joshua returned, still controlling his voice and his expression. But his eyes were watchful on Christy's face.

"You know I can't stay alone with you in your apartment. You can't expect it. It would be impossible, impossible—"

"Is it me you don't trust, or yourself?" said Joshua softly.

"Neither of us." Christy's face betrayed every bit of the anguish she felt at his suggestion. "Oh, *Joshua*—"

"Give in, Christy," he said in a tone that was like a touch, wooing her with his voice although he remained across the room. "You know you want to. You need me as much as I need you. How can you deny it after tonight? Lord help me, Christy, if you knew how much I need you...."

"Stop," she begged, "stop! I can't go to New York with you, not unless Mrs. Cousins goes, too. If you needed me so much you'd...." But she halted midway through the sentence. Though her pride was already in ruins after her volcanic response to Joshua, she still found enough of it to prevent her from mentioning marriage again.

There was no need, however. Joshua understood her. "Christy, I *can't*. Don't you understand? I don't want marriage. And I won't pretend I do, not even to get the thing I do want. Give me credit for honesty at least! I won't deceive you, as you deceived your fiancé just now—as he probably deceives you every Saturday night. If he cared enough he would have married you long before now, and to hell with plans and budgets. I don't believe he loves you."

And then, with a catch in her voice, Christy asked the question she had been wanting to ask: "Do *you*?"

Joshua raked his pale hair with those long, lean, powerful fingers—fingers whose touch still scorched her memory. His eyes wore a haunted look, and his voice was rough. "Oh, hell, Christy—don't ask. I'm not prepared to answer, for I won't lie. At this point in time all I have on my mind is bed. I'm damned if I'll let myself think about love until—" he paused and then grated out the admission "—until I've done something about my frustration. My God, I haven't slept with a woman for more than three years!"

8

CHRISTY STARED AT HIM with incredulity and growing pity as the meaning of his words became clear to her. "Joshua, you can't mean...? But your wife died only six months ago!"

He laughed, a bitter soul-rending sound that told of torment in a way that tears would never have done. "It's out now, Christy, so you may as well know the rest. Lana and I didn't live together as man and wife after... after she decided that Natalie's troubles were my fault. She hated me for that! Three years...three *years*, Christy, and I've never had the temperament of a monk. Not that the relationship had ever been satisfactory in any case. She managed to pretend a good deal more passion before marriage than she ever managed later. She was a cold woman, Christy. Cold and unloving. And I think before she died I hated her as much as it's possible to hate another human being. Do you think I can think about marriage after an experience like that?"

Christy said nothing. But her heart went across the room to the tall, gaunt, vehement man who paced the floor, revealing the horrors of his married life.

"When I married Lana, I had known her for only three months. And slept with her half a dozen times. It was an instant affair; good Lord, she practically dragged me into bed within hours of meeting her. She was a beautiful woman, exquisite, impeccable—it wasn't hard for her to do. And I'd never been a saint. Oh, it wasn't passion that motivated her, so it must have been that she decided I was a good catch. She claimed there was no possibility of pregnancy. It wasn't until later that she admitted she had lied."

Joshua clenched and unclenched his fists, then resumed his story, his voice now bleak. "I can't pretend I was pleased. I was still interning—a wife wasn't in my plans, especially one who had deceived me into marriage. Long before Natalie's birth I discovered that Lana was...cold. By then I had finished with interning; I was just starting my own practice. Things weren't entirely satisfactory for the first five years, but at least Lana worked at making the marriage a success. She had a need to be perfect: to do all the right things, to be seen in the right places, to choose the right clothes; in those things she could hardly be faulted. In being a mother, too—'parenting,' she used to call it; how I hate terms like that—she was a perfectionist. She used to talk interminably about Natalie's tiniest failings.

"There were things Lana and I disagreed about from the first. I wanted to practice on Nantucket; she hated it here. I preferred a simpler existence; she didn't. All the same it was a workable arrangement. Not happy, but then I threw myself into my work to compensate. And perhaps Natalie provided me with some of the warmth that the marriage didn't—she was always an affectionate child. Natalie had to go to a private school when the time came. On Nantucket I'd never have considered such a thing; in New York it's a virtual necessity. And frankly, Lana was anxious to put her into school by then, for Natalie was a constant reminder that human beings are less than perfect.

"The school spotted problems at once. Lana was called in for a conference. Some counselor thoughtlessly brought up the question of whether there might have been brain damage at birth...but I told you all about that.

"And why didn't I tell Lana to go to hell when she tried to attach the blame to me?" Joshua ran his hand around the back of his neck with such suppressed emotion that Christy longed to run to him across the room. "I suppose the main reason was that my wife seemed by then to be in a state of deep emotional crisis. She wouldn't consider a psychiatrist—for herself or for Natalie. To her that would have been admitting failure. I tried to insist, but she didn't want to listen, and my insistence only made things worse.

"I brought up divorce. But there was the custody problem. God, I couldn't let *her* have custody of Natalie! It would have been wrong for Natalie; I knew that. And even though Lana was refusing me her bed by then, she used to torment herself with thoughts that I might be in someone else's. She could be jealous, hysterical one moment—and the next she'd be throwing some other woman in my path, almost as though she wanted me to be unfaithful. And, dammit, I nearly was—a hundred times! I'm no plaster saint, and as my marriage had turned so sour. . . .

"But there was always the knowledge of Natalie to restrain me. I wanted to do nothing that would allow Lana leverage to get custody in any divorce action. I'm not sure how I existed—and resisted—through those years. It was hell, sheer hell.

"Natalie knew none of this; she was in school most of the time. Or in summer camp. And both Lana and I managed to put a good face on things when she was home. Matters might never have come to a head if I hadn't insisted that we do something about Natalie's problems. Finally, without Lana's knowledge, I made arrangements for the assessment. And then I told her.

"It was that last night, the night of the fire. I presented the thing to Lana as a fait accompli. I told her Natalie was to be admitted the following week, and that I was prepared to go ahead with it whether she liked it or not. It was a terrible scene. And it was then that she told me—told me that I had no right to interfere."

By now Joshua's long back was turned to Christy, and she could no longer see his face, but the corded tension of his shoulders and the hands balled into fists told her all she needed to know. Perhaps it was intuition, perhaps clues given in the earlier conversation, perhaps extrasensory perception, but Christy knew what he was going to say as surely as if he had already said it.

"She told me Natalie was not my child. She was hysterical, trying to strike back. It seemed unlikely, but I knew it *could* be true—Lana hadn't been a virgin when I first met her. No doubt she had had the odd affair because it was the bright, modern, smart thing to do. She told me there had been...others, not only before we married, but recently. To pay me back, she said, for *my* infidelities.

"Oh, I didn't think it was true, but can you imagine how I *felt*? I told her I'd be damned if I let myself be tied to a marriage in which there could be no trust—on either side. That I was going to be unfaithful at once, that night, and she was welcome to the evidence if she wanted it.... I can't even remember the things I said. I stormed out of the house. Lord knows what I might have done—I hardly know myself! But in the end I didn't do it. I had driven halfway to New York when I turned back; I knew that somehow I had to convince Lana to do the right thing for Natalie, whether she was my child or not. But it was too late when I got there. The house was ablaze, the housekeeper and the maid trapped on the third floor....

"What was it—accident or suicide? I don't know; I may never know. Lana was certainly mentally disturbed by then. She had taken a heavy dose of sleeping pills, it turned out. I didn't even know she had the wretched pills, but then I wasn't her doctor, and we weren't sharing a bedroom.

"I tried to get to the second floor. The stairs collapsed and I was trapped by a burning timber. I might as well have driven to New York for all the good it did. They all died...all of them. The housekeeper, the maid, Lana."

A heavy silence fell, a silence during which Joshua doubtless relived the purgatory of the fire. Finally Christy spoke in a low voice. "You can't blame yourself. You tried to save her, it might just as easily have happened some night when you were out on a call."

"Oh, God," he exploded bitterly, "do you really believe that? Lana was a sick woman—jealous, vindictive, capable of anything. But it's all in the past now. There's Natalie to think of...and those months in hospital made a lot of things come clear. I think Lana was lying, for one thing. And even if she wasn't—well, I don't give a damn who the natural father is. It isn't the act of conception that turns a man into a father; it's the actions that follow. The—what was it we talked about yesterday—the loving and giving. As far as Natalie's concerned, I love her as much as I ever did. More, if anything."

"Oh, Joshua." Christy longed to run to him, to throw herself into his arms, to comfort him with her hands and with her heart. But he did not want her heart. He wanted one thing only, one thing that was less than all of her; and less than all of herself was more than she was prepared to give. And yet compassion very nearly made her change her mind.

"Spare me your pity, Christy," he said tightly, as if he had read her thoughts. He had turned back to face her now, the gaunt features closed and composed. Joshua's ascetic self had taken over; the demons that drove him were for the moment under control. "I've told you all this because I wanted to explain to you . . . explain why I can't even think of a commitment right now, or perhaps for years. If ever! At this point in time what I need is to leap into bed, not marriage. Heaven knows, if anyone tempted me to offer more, it would be you. You'd make a good mother for Natalie. But that's not reason enough for marriage. Nor is frustration. And that's my main problem at the moment: frustration beyond anything you can imagine. I need a woman—and almost any woman will do."

Christy hugged her arms about herself, feeling suddenly ice-cold and empty. No, compassion was not reason enough to give herself to Joshua.

"I'll ask once more, Christy, and abide by your decision. Will you change your mind about New York?"

"No," she answered in a voice that could not have been her own.

Joshua's tone became curt and businesslike, as if it were he who had rebuffed her. "I suppose it's too late to apologize for trying to talk you into an affair, when it's obviously not your style. My only excuse is the extremity of my need—it's made me behave in irrational ways. I can see I've made your life uncomfortable by attempting to vent my frustrations on you. And there's no need, when. . . ."

The thought remained unspoken, although his next words made it clear. He stalked toward the door of the library. "I'll take Mrs. Cousins with me to baby-sit Natalie. I'd prefer you didn't come at all, under the circumstances. Perhaps when I return I won't be so . . . so damn frustrated that I can't even think straight. Then I can start sorting out how I feel about things. Good night, Christy."

9

ON WEDNESDAY the world turned all gold again, as if to make amends for Tuesday's weeping skies. Christy had been teaching Natalie to ride a bike, and today, at last, the little girl had caught the knack of it. Delighted with her new prowess, she had begged to go farther afield. Lessons, and the beach in front of Graydunes, had been abandoned for the day. Christy and Natalie had taken a picnic lunch to the Children's Beach near the town of Nantucket, where there was a lifeguard on duty and the diversion of other children. It was quite late when they returned home, and so it was near suppertime when Christy learned of the onward march of events, from Mrs. Cousins.

The housekeeper had been waiting for their return, and she was evidently in a state of flurry.

"Run to the library at once, Natalie—your father wants to see you. No, don't bother about shaking the sand out of your shoes. Hurry now! He said to send you along the moment you got in—and I shouldn't wonder if he had something special to tell you."

When Natalie had vanished, Mrs. Cousins turned to Christy. "Lands sakes, that phone's been ringing all day—hardly a moment's peace! Dr. Joshua got a phone call this morning from a doctor friend in New York, and ever since the wires have been burning up between here and there. We're flying to New York tomorrow—I know I don't need to explain to you, Christy, for he told me you knew what it was all about. Natalie's to have some tests done, starting Friday. Of course you can't go, for your young man's coming. Dr. Joshua says you'll be staying here. But I have bad news for you, Christy."

"Bad news?"

"Yes—and I hardly know how to tell you! I never thought it of Dr. Joshua, that he'd be so old-fashioned! He says your young man's not to stay at Graydunes after all."

"I see." Was it relief or annoyance that flooded through Christy? She hardly knew; for although she was less than enthusiastic about the idea of staying alone with David, she felt that Joshua had no right to lay down rules for her behavior. Especially when he had implied, only last night, that he had every intention of putting an end to his own frustrations while he was in New York.

"Even I'm not that old-fashioned," Mrs. Cousins was going on, "and I told him so. Told him it was none of his business—but he was very short with me about that! Though I suppose it's his house, if the truth be told, and he has the right to say who'll stay here and who won't. Personally I can't see who'd think twice about it, except Tom Maybee, and he's off to Madaket for the weekend, to stay with his sister, and won't be back till next Tuesday. But don't worry, Christy: Dr. Joshua has found a place for your young man to put up, with some friends of his in town. They run a guesthouse, and it won't cost you a cent, for Dr. Joshua has agreed to pay out of his own pocket. Says you have it coming to you, for he's never paid you extra for doing the nanny's job. Now don't open your mouth to complain, for it's all arranged! And David's to have the use of the Chevrolet, too—so you can't find fault with the doctor's generosity. I expect he has your best interests at heart."

Or his own best interests, Christy thought with a surge of irritation. But at the moment she let none of her mixed reactions show, and said to Mrs. Cousins with a deceptive lightness, "I expect he does. It's very good of him to offer the car. David and I can do some sight-seeing. There are parts of the island I'd like to visit without having to pedal all the way."

"Well, you'll have a good chance now. It's time you had a few days off."

"Did Dr. Joshua say how long you'd be staying in New York?" asked Christy with studied casualness.

"A week. We'll be back next Friday—and I expect it will almost be like a holiday for me, too! Nobody to cook for half the time, for Dr. Joshua said he's planning to eat out most nights, at least the nights Natalie's in the hospital. He's been on the phone half the day— Oh, drat, there it goes again!" The shrill sound of the telephone interrupted her words, and she started to wipe floury hands on her apron. "Dr. Joshua said I was to answer it while he's talking to Natalie— Oh, can you get it, Christy? I'm bound to leave a trail of flour all over the floor, and I've just washed it. Take a message. He said he was expecting news about some theater tickets."

By the time Christy reached the phone, it was ringing for the fourth time. Evidently Joshua, in the library, had become impatient with its insistence. He must have already said hello, for what Christy heard was a female voice on the other end—a voice that sounded breathless and excited, and only too familiar.

"Joshua, darling, how good to get your message! I thought you'd never—"

But whatever Doris Moody had never thought, Christy didn't wait to find out. She replaced the receiver quietly. "He answered," she told Mrs. Cousins without elaboration, but the confirmation of Joshua's plans for New York left her with a cold feeling in the pit of her stomach. Joshua in that voluptuous, willing embrace; Joshua's silvery hair mingling with a tangle of auburn; Joshua's mouth passionately parting those sultry lips.... And yet why should she care? She had made her decision, hadn't she? A decision that did not include temporary interludes of the type Joshua had in mind.

She saw Joshua twice more before he left for New York. The first occasion was that same night, at the evening meal. In the presence of Natalie, the conversation revolved around the happenings of the coming week as they affected the child. Natalie was apprehensive, understandably, and Christy had to admit that Joshua's matter-of-fact manner went a long way toward putting the child's fears to rest. He handled it well, explaining what must be explained in a straightforward way, and saying nothing that would add to Natalie's alarm. The prospect of a special night at the theater—tickets had been procured, heaven knew how, for a suitable smash-hit musical—distracted Natalie somewhat. And so did another promise: a promise to take her digging for quahogs, with Christy, sometime after the return from New York. By bedtime the child seemed to be almost eager for the coming trip.

It was the following day, just before the small group left for the airport, that Christy saw Joshua alone.

The travelers were already bundling into the Jeep, for Old Tom was driving them to the airport. Christy, casually clad in shorts and halter top, was standing on the front steps to wave goodbye. The phone rang, and she ran back into the house to answer.

It was for Joshua, long distance from New York. Only a florist wanting to check on an address—but it was enough that Christy had to race to the front door and signal him back from the car.

"Tell them to hold on," called Joshua, who was still adjusting suitcases to make room for passengers. "I'll be there in a minute."

Christy did as he asked, hurriedly, so that she might escape back to the front steps before he had time to come inside the house. But she had hardly finished relaying the message when Joshua himself arrived in the library. He caught her by the wrist, his grip insistent, drawing her back to the telephone while he spoke into it for a brief moment. The address confirmed, he hung up.

"Please let me go," begged Christy, desperately trying to free herself from his shackling grasp. He only drew her closer, and his other hand, now freed from the telephone, captured her shoulder.

"Christy...you can still change your mind. Come with me. We've twenty minutes to spare before the flight."

"Oh, Joshua, don't ask! Don't make it so difficult for me." Her voice was anguished. His sudden insistence had caught her with her guard down, for she had thought herself safe by now. "Don't you see I can't—"

But his mouth came down over hers, stopping the next words in her throat. As her lips parted to permit the invasion, he grew hungry and probing in his demands. Christy didn't hold back. Pride was forgotten; caution was abandoned; resolutions reached painfully were thrown to the winds. She clung to Joshua, her lips wildly responsive, her slim curves melting against his greater height. Their mouths moved in unison, tongues exploring as they had explored so often before—but this time with a tenderness that was a wonderment in itself. The taste of him, the texture of him, the touch of him brought back all the sensuous experience she had gained during those past weeks, so that when his hands began to adventure, she made no move to stop him.

His strong fingers slid to the back edges of her shorts, seductively tracing the lower line of the curve they barely concealed. A low moan came to her lips. She murmured into the corner of his mouth, "Oh, Joshua, Joshua...."

His warm breath mingled with hers, filling her mouth. "Christy, darling...darling. Come with me. I want you so."

Temptation rose like a great wind, sweeping through her, sweeping reason away. And suddenly her hands were urgent around his neck, drawing him closer, telling him that she wanted him, too, telling him everything he wanted to know, telling him that she was willing to forfeit the future for a stolen moment of the present. "Oh, yes, Joshua, yes...."

And if, at that moment, there had been no others to consider, no flight to catch, no plans to alter, possibly her willingness would have become wantonness. But at her words Joshua pulled away, his gaze warm upon her flushed face. His eyes blazed with triumph and passion, caressing her, possessing her, turning her limbs to liquid.

"Come on, then, Christy. Don't even pack; I'll buy you everything you need in New York."

"I'll have to change. I can't go in shorts," protested Christy. Her pulses were still racing, her head in a spin from the impetuosity of the decision—but even in the confusion of the moment she knew her clothing was totally unsuitable for a flight to New York.

"Change, then, but hurry. I'll tell Mrs. Cousins that you're going in her place.... Oh, darling, you won't regret this. I'll make it good for you, I promise."

But reality, once given a toehold, came thundering back in full force. There was David to consider: how had she so nearly forgotten him?

"Oh, Joshua—" Her falling face told of inner struggles; told him that his victory had not yet been won. "There's David."

He frowned impatiently. "Tom Maybee can meet him at the airport tomorrow and explain. Forget him, Christy. You can't change your mind now. Oh, darling. . . ."

And he made as if to gather her in his arms again, but Christy pulled right away, for the moment of weakness had passed. "That's right—I can't change my mind now. I won't go to New York, Joshua."

"Christy—"

"No, Joshua. It's too late." Even now, the honking of a horn outside told that the occupants of the Jeep were becoming worried about catching the flight.

"Oh, *hell!* Let them wait. Christy, you must—"

"You'll miss your flight, Joshua. *That* won't wait." Some of her anguish at sending him into another woman's arms must have showed in her face. "Go, Joshua," she said in a low tone. "Just go."

But he would not give up so easily. He caught at Christy's hand, capturing her slender fingers in a grip of steel. "I won't go until you promise you'll let me take you out to dinner when I come back. Next Friday night."

"Joshua, I can't."

"*Promise.*"

"Whatever it is you're looking for, I'm sure you'll. . . you'll find it in New York." Her throat hurt to say the words.

"To hell with my plans for New York. I've made no plans I can't change. I'd rather be with you. Dinner next Friday, Christy."

The honking was becoming more insistent, and because it seemed easy to promise, easier than remaining like this, with Joshua's hand pressing urgent messages into hers, Christy said the words he wanted to hear.

"All right, then, I promise."

"Hold David off a little longer—and make that a promise, too."

She nodded, unable to trust herself to speak.

Joshua pulled her close for one more breathless moment. "Wait for me, Christy," he whispered huskily into her hair. "Lord knows, I can wait, too. . . ." And he kissed her again, a brief possessive kiss that sealed the pact. Then he was gone. . .and it was some moments before it came to Christy just exactly what she had promised; what Joshua would *think* she had promised. He had said he would change his own plans for New York, and she had allowed him to say it. He had asked her to wait; he had said he would wait; but for what? By implication, what she had promised Joshua for next Friday included far more than a dinner. . . .

She buried her face in her hands and gave in to tears, a slow steady flow that lasted until there were no more tears to shed; lasted until long past the time when Joshua's flight to New York had safely landed. It was as well there was nobody around today but Old Tom— and Old Tom, as always kept to himself in the apartment over the garage, and Christy hardly knew he was there.

"AIN'T NO TROUBLE," Old Tom told her the next afternoon. "Doc Josh told me I was to pick up your young feller at the airport, an' show him the guesthouse where he's to shack up, an' drop his bags there. Mighty concerned he seemed, too, that it be done before I aimed off to my sister Martha's." He gave Christy a bland blue glance that told her he was quite in accordance with "Doc Josh" in his concern for Christy's moral welfare. "Then, an' only then, I'm to give your fee-ancee the keys for the Chevy. Fact is, Doc Josh, he tried to get me to think twice about spending the weekend over Madaket way. But I ain't able to do that, for it's a family reunion, an' there's others to be taken into mind."

Christy pushed aside a moment of annoyance. What right had Joshua to decide she needed chaperoning, when his own plans for New York had so evidently included exactly the kind of thing he wanted her not to do? But there was no point taking her resentment out on Old Tom, so she tried to put a cheerful face on things.

"I'm sure Dr. Joshua needn't worry about me. I can take care of myself. And there's no need for you to go to the airport. I told David to take a taxi. As it's not a scheduled flight, it's impossible to say exactly when he'll arrive. He could be quite late."

"Well, now...." Old Tom stopped to think about that, then shook his head. "Not too keen to be late at Martha's, I'll admit. But who's to show him where the guesthouse is but me?"

"He could go there by taxi," Christy suggested, "on his way here. He'll be phoning from the airport, and I could give him the address. A taxi driver would be able to find the place, surely?"

"Ayeh, that's so." Old Tom considered her suggestion with a slow scratch of his ear. "Well, now, I'll think on it. We'll wait an' see what time your feller phones. Could be he'll come in bright an' early, an' then it's no trouble, not a bit of it. That's what we'll do. Ayeh. Wait an' see."

But David did not arrive early, and long before his phone call came, Old Tom had been champing at the bit, eager to reach his sister's in time for the family gathering. With some reluctance and a few last-minute words of moralizing, he gave Christy the address of the guesthouse and the keys to the Chevrolet, and took off across the island in the battered old Jeep.

B-ringgg. B-ringgg. B-ringgg. Christy picked up the receiver, relieved that the call had finally come.

"Hello?"

"Christy! We're here. Just landed."

"Oh, David.... Did you have a good flight?"

"Swell, thanks. I can hardly wait to see you. Did you manage to lay it on for that gardener to pick me up? Or do I have to spring for a taxi?"

"Sorry, David. You'll have to take a taxi."

"Oh, damn. Well, maybe Lenny's folks can give me a lift—or rather, his chauffeur."

"Lenny?"

"The friend with the plane. His folks are vacationing on Nantucket; they own a big summer estate over near Wauwinet. He phoned them just now, and they're sending a car to the airport."

"Wauwinet's the opposite direction from Graydunes, David. You can't ask. It would be an imposition."

"Can't I, now?" David's voice became teasing on the other end of the line. "Aren't you the little Miss Proper! Give me directions to Graydunes anyway, Christy, just in case I need them."

She knew then that David would do as he pleased, and she gave him the directions without enthusiasm. "But, David—"

"Yes? Hurry up, Christy. Lenny's waiting to use the phone again. He wants to check in with his date for tonight."

"You can't stay here—you can't stay at Graydunes." There, it was out; and David's reaction was just as angry as she had known it would be. She broke through the flood of protests that crackled across the line and explained about the guesthouse and the Chevrolet. She omitted only the reasons for the change in plans.

"Well, at least it won't cost anything," grumbled David once he realized his complaints would gain him nothing. "And the car will come in handy. All the same, I can't see why—"

"Have the taxi take you to the guesthouse before you come out," Christy broke in, and gave him the address. "I have the Chevrolet keys for you, David. And...I've made reservations for a late dinner, at a restaurant in town."

Again a swearword. "Christy, we can't afford it!"

"My treat," she said as breezily as possible. "Now you'd better get off the phone, hadn't you? I'll see you soon."

It was some time before David arrived—far longer than the trip from the airport necessitated, even with a side trip into the town of Nantucket. When he arrived Christy was already hovering near the front door of Graydunes, becomingly dressed for the evening in a floaty dress of soft Indian cotton, printed in blacks and browns and natural tones. It was already past dusk. Not wanting David to know she was alone at Graydunes, she had switched on many more lights than necessary for a large house with only a single occupant. She had also turned on a radio in the library, the sound of which carried through the main floor.

David arrived not in a taxi but in a long sleek chauffeur-driven Cadillac. It discharged its passenger and purred away into the gathering darkness.

Christy opened the front door and found herself caught in a warm embrace.

"Christy, honey—" David's mouth came down, claiming hers. The masculine taste of him mingled with the faint flavor of alcohol. He had stopped somewhere for a drink, probably with his friend Lenny. She felt nothing, nothing at all, not even the warm accepting sense of enjoyment she used to feel at his touch. David was good-looking in a purposeful way, all drive and determination, the type of man who would never want for female companionship. Yet at the moment she wondered why she had ever thought herself in love with him. She extricated herself from his embrace, covering the moment with a light laugh.

"You'll ruin my makeup, David!"

"You've never worried about makeup before. Let's look at you, Christy. Hey—you do look tired. So it was the flu, was it?"

"Just a touch," she lied. "I'm fine now. Shall we go?"

David looked around, taking in the broad sweep of stairway, the luxurious carpeting, the antiques that were visible through the living-room door. In that room, as elsewhere, there were lamps switched on. A sliver of light showed beneath the door to the library, and strains of the 1812 Overture spilled into the hall.

"Aren't you going to introduce me to your Dr. Brent?" Then David's voice grew lower, conspiratorial. "I've been asking around about him, Christy. He's got quite a reputation—he could be a big help to me."

"Er, he hates to be interrupted, David. And he's still not too well."

David shrugged away his disappointment. "Ah, well. Tomorrow's time enough. Aren't you going to invite me in? I could use a drink. Or are you forbidden the use of the liquor cabinet?"

"No to both questions, David. But I made a reservation for nine o'clock. We'll have to hurry or we'll lose our table. Friday night in the height of the season, the restaurant will be jammed." She handed him the car keys from her purse. "Did your friend's chauffeur have any trouble finding the guesthouse?"

"No, for we didn't go there." And then, as they walked toward the garage, he explained why. Christy noted with some satisfaction that Tom Maybee had left a light burning in the apartment above the garage: another evidence of habitation. And inside the garage there were still two cars to give the place a lived-in look. Perhaps the weekend would not be too difficult after all, especially with what David was telling her now.

"Lenny's folks wouldn't hear of my staying in a guesthouse. Moved me right in, bag and baggage. That's what took so long; I went directly there from the airport. Quite a spread they have! Tennis courts, swimming pool, servants coming out of the woodwork.... Well, I always knew Lenny's family was well fixed, but it's a revelation all the same, how the other half lives. Quite a swinging crowd, too. Big party planned for later tonight, ten o'clock on. We're invited to drop in after dinner."

"Oh?" said Christy without enthusiasm.

"I told them we'd be there. Too bad it wasn't a dinner party; we could have saved the price of this little outing."

"Oh, David—do we always have to talk about the budget? Please, just for once—"

"Just for once what?" he asked with a frown as they got into the Chevrolet. "What's eating you, Christy?"

"Just enjoy," she finished lamely, knowing even as she said it that it was something she could not do herself, not tonight. "Remember it's my treat. Forget about money for tonight."

David laughed, a little apologetically, and started the car. "Sorry, honey. You're right. But it's one of those things. Until you get it, it's hard to forget it. Someday we'll have so much we'll be wallowing in it, like Lenny's folks. Do you know, they have *two* yachts?"

Oh, what was the use, thought Christy—had David always been like this, or was she just seeing him with different eyes? David's parents had died when he was quite young, and it had been a struggle for him to afford medical school. Summer jobs, part-time jobs, penny-pinching. Once that fierce determination to succeed had attracted her to him. But had David lost something along the way—a humanity that Joshua still had? Joshua: she mustn't let herself think of Joshua. There was no future with Joshua. But nor, she knew now, was there a future with David. She had known the decision would become easy as soon as she saw him again; and now the decision was made. It only remained to tell David. And as dinner ended, over coffee and tiny thimblefuls of Tia Maria, she knew she could not put it off much longer.

He had already told her of his plans for setting up practice, plans that were coming closer with every passing month. She had told him of a job offer recently received, the belated result of an interview conducted before coming to Nantucket. "But I don't want to work in another boarding school, David. I feel I want to—"

"Want to what? The salary sounds good enough."

"I want to be freer, that's all," Christy commented, but the truth was that at this moment she wanted to make no commitments for the future. "And maybe I'll find something better in September."

And now David was broaching the subject that made it impossible for her to stall any longer.

"When your parents come back, Christy, we can start thinking about a wedding date. It should be done right. Your folks can certainly afford it, with only one daughter to marry off and your brothers already settled into married life. I'd like the proper trimmings." His voice lowered, became intimate; and in the dim candlelight of the restaurant his hand came across the table and closed over hers. "Except the white dress, darling." His meaning was clear. "Christy...."

She forced her hand to remain beneath his, for she wanted no scenes in this crowded place. With a bright noncommittal smile she suggested, "Let's ask for the bill, David, and leave. Didn't you say that party started at ten?"

"Do you really want to go to the party right away?" His tone held worlds of meaning.

"No. No, I don't," Christy confessed, although her reasons were not the same as his.

"Neither do I. I'd rather find a quiet beach," he said in a disturbing voice. "We can always join the party later—I gather it's likely to go on for all hours. I told you, Lenny's quite a swinger. And so are his friends."

He signaled the waiter, and moments later they were out in the fresh night air, finding their way to the Chevrolet, which was parked on a quiet side street lined with weathered frame houses pressing up against the sidewalk.

Christy allowed herself to be helped into the passenger seat. But as soon as David moved into place beside her, she procrastinated no longer. Nothing could make this scene easier—especially not a secluded stretch of beach. It must be said: and it might as well be said here, in the half-sleeping town, in the relative privacy of the car.

"Wait, David. Don't start the car yet."

His hand remained poised over the ignition key, and Christy went on hastily, allowing him no time to answer.

"I don't want to marry you, David."

In the half-light of the streetlamp she could see his dumbfounded expression as he turned to face her, leaving the key unturned. "Christy—what the hell kind of joke is that?"

"It's not a joke, David. I can't marry you. I don't love you. Perhaps I never did, or at least not enough. Oh, I'm very fond of you, but—"

"But what?" he interjected, a mixture of anger and disbelief darkening his face. "What is this, Christy—cold feet again? I got the impression you had agreed to...plan ahead."

"I...." She looked at him with a silent plea, wishing he would do something to make this easier for him. "I didn't say that. You misunderstood."

"Why can't you just admit you lost your nerve? Dammit, Christy—"

"That has nothing to do with it, David, nothing at all. I just don't love you. The spark isn't there anymore."

He gave a ragged laugh. "Was it ever? You've never given me a proper chance to show what I can do. Christy—" And he turned his body, reaching for her, capturing her despite her efforts to evade him. His hands pinioned her arms and his mouth sought hers hungrily.

"No, David, no—"

But he drowned her protests with the ferocity of his kiss, a kiss that held passion but no gentleness. The kiss numbed Christy and left David, several minutes later, breathing heavily. He seemed not to notice that she had not responded, only submitted.

"Sparks don't fly without friction, Christy," he murmured huskily into her hair. "We haven't seen enough of each other. Oh, God, you're so soft...." He eased his grip on her arms, and moved his hand toward her breast.

Now, with her arms freed, she was able to push at his chest. "David, don't you understand? I don't want you...I don't love you. There's nothing there, nothing. I can't marry you."

"Christy, we've made *plans*."

"Plans can change, but I can't. I can't marry someone who, who...." *Leaves me cold*, she wanted to say. But it was too unkind, and it had not always been true; so she said instead, "Someone who's just become a habit with me. It's no good, David. We're through."

Carefully he disengaged his arms and settled back into his own space, his hands resting on the steering wheel, his scowl aimed out into the night. He remained silent for some moments, and Christy knew what he was thinking about.

"The money's all in your name, David," she said at last, knowing it would be difficult for him to broach the subject. "I don't give a damn about it."

"You earned most of it," he said stiffly. "I have some pride."

"You'll need it to set up practice. I don't mind."

"Well, I do," he said fiercely through gritted teeth. "I've clawed my way up this far. I'll take what I can, where I can, but I'm not accepting charity from you."

"It's not charity, David. Consider it a loan if you prefer."

"I can just as easily get a bank loan—and frankly, I'd rather." And then, becoming almost savage, he grated at her, "You don't think I need you to help me make my way up the ladder, do you? I'll get to the top, Christy—with you or without you."

"I'm sure you will, David," she returned, feeling exhausted. The strain sounded in her voice. "And I'll be glad for you, really I will. But I don't want to join you on the way up."

"What made you change your mind?" Bitterness, anger, betrayal—they made his voice that of a stranger, hard and hateful.

"There's another man."

"Someone who makes sparks fly?" he retorted sarcastically.

"Yes, David. The way they should have been flying with us. I realize it now. I'm sorry."

"I see." Again, a few moments of silence. Then, as if seeking his own pound of flesh, he gritted, "I won't pretend there haven't been other women. Nurses are a dime a dozen, and there's always a cheap floozy or two wanting to snag a doctor for a husband. You didn't think I was saving myself for you, did you?"

"No, David, I didn't." Tiredness, tiredness. "Please, David, take me home."

He ignored the request. "Who is it—this Dr. Brent? Is that why I couldn't stay there? Why you didn't want to introduce me tonight?"

"I didn't say it was Dr. Brent." She sidestepped the issue, but none too neatly, for David's suspicions remained in his next words.

"Did you decide that he's a better catch than me? No wonder you're not interested in joining me on my way up the ladder. Why start at the bottom when you can start at the top! God, Christy—"

"Oh, *David!*" she burst through his words. Why did he insist on imputing his own motives to other people? And yet she had known he would be hurt and angry, and perhaps wanting to strike back at her. David was not one to give in easily. "Dr. Brent's not the only man on Nantucket," she reminded him. "And even if he were, he'd hardly be one to set my cap for. He's barely over his wife's death."

"Sometimes that's the easiest catch. A lonely

widower, and already broken in to harness—with a young daughter to boot. I'm not a fool, Christy! What other man have you had time to see?"

"Stop it, David! It's not Joshua—not Dr. Brent."

He turned to look at her, his face harsh and disbelieving and resentful. "Introduce me to him when we get to Graydunes, then. It's still early. He's likely to be up."

Christy steepled her hands and pressed them to her face, willing the moment to end. David was stubborn, she had always known that; it was part of what had given him the drive to get through medical school against all odds. It was one of his strengths, one of the things she had once thought she loved. And now he wanted to punish her for letting him down. In this case he would gain nothing by persevering, but Christy knew he would persevere all the same. And she could not admit now that there was no one at Graydunes, so reluctantly she confessed. "All right, David. You win. I can't introduce you. It *is* Dr. Brent."

"So I'm right," scowled David. "Money talks! The carrot on the stick—has he offered marriage yet?"

"No," said Christy tiredly. "And he never will. Now can we please leave, David? I want to go home."

"Of course you've slept with him, or you wouldn't be so sure about his sexual attractions." David twisted the ignition key viciously. "How could you give yourself so cheaply, Christy—after holding me at arm's length for all those years? *How could you?*"

It was pointless to deny anything, and in the end perhaps only more damaging to David's self-esteem. So the drive back to Graydunes was accomplished in uncomfortable silence. When he braked by the front door of Graydunes, he finally broke the silence.

"I won't see you again while I'm here—you know that, don't you? I'll be at Lenny's if you need me." He gave her the address. "I'll use this car tonight because I have no choice. I'll make arrangements to get it back to Graydunes tomorrow or Sunday. I'm sure the chauffeur will oblige by tailing me out here and giving me a lift back to Lenny's."

Christy mumbled an appropriate answer.

"When I do bring it," David went on, "I'll leave it in the garage, key in the ignition." His voice became heavily sarcastic. "You don't mind if I don't stop in to say hello at the time, do you? I don't think I can stand all those flying sparks."

"Perhaps that's best. I may be out somewhere, anyway."

"So long, Christy. It's been nice knowing you." His final salutation was abrupt and unpleasant. "Tell Dr. Brent no thanks for everything."

"Can't we part friends? It's been so many years."

"Oh, *damn*, Christy—you don't expect me to be a good sport about the whole thing, do you? Smile and say 'best of luck'? A man has some pride. Oh, I know I've been behaving badly, but it's not just because you've thrown all my plans for a loop. If I hadn't cared about you, really cared about you, you wouldn't have been part of my plans at all."

"I know that." She stretched a hand out to touch his whitened knuckles against the steering wheel. "I *did* care about you, David. But not as much as I should have."

With what seemed a great effort, he forced his grip to relax a little and turned his head in her direction. "Don't bother saying you're sorry, Christy. I don't think I could bear that."

She opened the car door. "I won't then. Good night, David, and . . . ."

"And?" he said pointedly, when she had stood for too

long, hesitant, wondering if she had burned too many bridges.

"Goodbye," she managed to say at last, closing the car door. Then, remembering, she removed the platinum-and-diamond engagement ring and handed it back to him, without comment, through the window. "Goodbye and good luck."

"Luck is something I've never counted on," he said viciously, and he was gone in a screech of tires on gravel.

10

It was what Old Tom Maybee said that gave her the idea. Old-fashioned Tom, with his roses and his arthritis and his sister Martha "over Madaket way," and his family reunion that didn't work out quite as planned. Or perhaps, to be more exact, it was what Old Tom didn't say, for the next time Christy spoke to him, midway through the following week, his conversation consisted of exactly one word.

She had kept to herself over the weekend, avoiding all contact with a world that seemed to have tumbled down around her ears. She had made the impossible choice—a choice not for Joshua, and not for David, but for neither. She could not marry David, considering how she felt about Joshua. Nor could she have an affair with Joshua: she still wanted a permanence he was not willing to promise. His return on Friday would face her with the dreadful necessity of keeping him at arm's length— of informing him that she would have no part of the affair he so urgently desired. Yet how could she convince him of that, with the implications of their last conversation? How could she trust him not to press his advantage, when she could hardly trust herself?

If it had not been for Natalie, Christy might at this point have left Nantucket altogether. But she could not abandon Natalie, not with a month of summer yet to go, and with the child just beginning to come out of the shell she had built to protect herself against a world that had thought her slow-witted. Depending on what happened in New York, Christy knew that Natalie might need her more than ever during the coming month.

And so might Joshua...but his was a need she was not prepared to meet. Christy tried, in part, to counterbalance her last reckless words to him by phoning long-distance to New York on Saturday morning. The operator had no difficulty putting her through. It seemed that Joshua was not one of those doctors who maintain an unlisted home number. The conversation was short and inconclusive, and thoroughly unsatisfactory. Joshua had answered, and had told Christy at once that Natalie's tests were already under way.

"That's good," she answered, suddenly hesitant to say what she had called about.

"I'm counting the days, Christy." His voice came soft and warm and intimate over the line—intimate in a way that turned Christy's insides to fluid.

"Please don't," she begged. "And don't change your plans for New York. Forget our last conversation."

"A promise is a promise." There was a harder edge to his voice now; she could almost imagine the corners of his fine mouth tightening. "A dinner engagement—is that so difficult?"

"I want you to release me. Or at least to remember that I promised nothing beyond dinner."

"I'm aware of that." Then, changing the subject abruptly, "How's David?"

"He's fine."

"Is he there right now?" It was nine o'clock in the morning; Christy knew why Joshua was asking.

"No."

"That ring doesn't suit you, you know."

"So you said. I remember." But she could not tell him

she had given it back: that would only encourage Joshua's expectations.

"Well, then." There was a moment's pause, and Joshua's voice again, now crisp and businesslike. "See you Friday," he said, and hung up.

Later, in midafternoon, Christy heard car sounds outside. A glimpse out the window told her that the Chevrolet was being returned, and not by David, but by a workman of some sort. The limousine, following closely, picked up the driver and vanished, leaving silence behind.

But it was a silence soon broken, for it was only a short time later that Christy heard the Jeep rattling along the drive and into the garage. This time she did not need to look. Old Tom had returned unexpectedly; the sounds of the Jeep were quite distinctive. Later she was to find out that it had been arthritis, a painful attack, that dragged him away from Saturday's gathering. But at the moment she did not know the reason, and, wallowing in her own misery, she did not particularly care. Old Tom's comings and goings were the least of her concerns at this point.

It was not until she saw him to speak to him, late Tuesday afternoon, that she learned he had been in his rooms over the garage all the time. She had gone outside to the rose garden for the first time in days. . .and there he was, bending over his bushes. With a small sense of surprise, she realized she had not heard the Jeep since the other day, although there had been other cars—a grocery delivery, a man to read some meter, a stranger asking directions.

"Why, Tom! Didn't you stay at your sister's after all? I heard you come in Saturday—have you been here ever since?"

"Ayeh." But he kept his back stubbornly turned, inviting no further conversation.

"Why did you come back? You weren't sick, I hope."

No answer. Something was bothering Old Tom—he had not been this uncommunicative since that first day, the day she had arrived by ferry.

"Has your arthritis been troubling you?" she tried again.

After a pause: "Ayeh."

Then she began to guess what might be upsetting him. The Chevrolet had been in the garage ever since Saturday. Did he think David had been staying at Graydunes, too? If so, he would probably assume the worst; and as Mrs. Cousins had said, Old Tom was old-fashioned. "I guess you're wondering—wondering why we didn't use the car, David and I."

Again the answer was slow in coming, and none too friendly when it did. "Ayeh."

"David didn't need it after all. Or the room at the guesthouse. He stayed with a friend."

Now Tom Maybe looked up for the first time, and his pale blue gaze was decidedly disapproving. Clearly he did not believe her. "Ayeh," he said with a total absence of credulity, and turned back to his rosebushes.

Christy felt the color rising to her face. "He hasn't been staying here," she said; but to that Old Tom replied not at all.

It was evident that he thought she had allowed David to stay at the house in open defiance of Joshua's express orders. If so, he must believe that David had left by taxi—that one of the other cars in the driveway earlier that day had been a cab. She opened her mouth to expand on the facts, then thought better of it. She had already told him the truth, and he had not believed her. There was no point in protesting further. In fact, to protest too much would only seem to confirm his suspi-

cions. So she turned away, putting an end to her efforts
at conversation.

No doubt she had not heard the last of it. Joshua was
sure to be told. Tom Maybee was loyal, and he would
not approve of such carryings-on, engagement or no
engagement, especially when "Doc Josh" was clearly
against it. But if the others wanted the truth she could
always tell them where David had been staying; she still
remembered the address.

But did she want to tell Joshua the truth—that she had
broken up with David? Ruefully she looked at her ring
finger and the band of untanned skin that told all too
plainly what had transpired during these past few days.
David was her last defense against Joshua, her only
defense. And that—that and Old Tom's disbelief and
disapproval—was what gave her the idea.

The following day she found what she was looking
for, in the town of Nantucket, in a small antique store.
It was a simple wide gold band with a chased pattern
nearly worn through by age—hardly showy, but a great
deal more affordable than the rings she had priced in the
jewelry store. It needed no adjustment. She bought it,
and soon the pale mark on her ring finger was covered.
Tom Maybee's objections would be put to an end, and
with luck Joshua's urgings, too. Of course, she would
still have to explain the absence of the engagement ring,
but that should not be hard.

And now, armored against Joshua, she faced Friday
night with a little more equanimity. To live the lie for
the next month would be hard, but it would not be as
hard as living the month without it.

Yet, if she had foreseen how awful it would be—that
moment when Joshua learned of her fabrication—would
she have bought the wedding band?

On Friday Natalie came bursting through the door

clutching parcels, followed closely by Mrs. Cousins. Last night had been the night of the musical, and Joshua had taken the child out for dinner as an added treat. This morning there had been some last-minute shopping at a truly marvelous New York toy store...and these were the things that became the first topics of conversation. The bubble of excitement lasted all the way up the stairs, while Christy helped Natalie to her room with her new acquisitions. After that, for a few minutes, Christy heard about the stay in hospital. Natalie had not liked all aspects of the testing, but on the whole she was quite content. The week had confirmed Christy's guesses, and it was evident Natalie found it a relief to know that her problems were neither unique nor insoluble. Perceptual handicaps had been explained to her in simple terms.

"Thomas Edison had one," Natalie exclaimed proudly, "and he was smart. So did somebody named Einstein, but I don't know who he was. I didn't mind the tests, either, most of them. Most of them were like games. But some of the other tests—ugh! The worst was the time when they took blood out of my finger, like this." Natalie took Christy's hand to demonstrate, and immediately her attention was distracted. "You have a new ring! What's this one for?"

"Something exciting happened to me, too, Natalie, while you were away," returned Christy in a light tone that in no way conveyed how wretched she felt to be lying to a small child. "I got married. This is a wedding ring."

"Christy! You *didn't*," came the answer in open-mouthed astonishment.

"Yes, I did. Last Saturday. You knew I was planning to get married, Natalie. David and I just decided we were tired of waiting, that's all." Christy sat down on the edge of Natalie's bed, as much for support as anything. Her legs felt shaky.

Natalie's purple eyes inspected her solemnly. "You don't look married. You look just the same."

"It's not how you look that's important," Christy gave an uncertain laugh. "It's how you feel." And how did she feel? Awful, awful, awful.

"Do I have to call you Mrs. now?"

"No, just Christy, same as always."

A disturbing thought occurred to Natalie. "Does this mean you'll be going away? I don't want you to go and live somewhere else—but of course you'll have to, won't you?" Her face began to crumple. "You'll be leaving."

"No, I won't be leaving," Christy said quickly. "At least not yet. I'll be staying here for the rest of the summer, just as I always planned. Eventually, of course, I'll have to go to my husband. He wouldn't like it if I stayed here too long."

"Oh, Christy, I want you to stay here forever." Natalie's thin arms went around Christy's neck, and the small brunette head burrowed itself against an encircling arm. Perhaps it was as well, for it meant that Natalie saw none of what followed in the next minute.

"Why, forever is too long, Natalie. Even you won't stay on Nantucket forever." As Christy said the words, a small movement caught her eye, and she looked up. Joshua was standing in the doorway, a smile crinkling at the corners of his eyes and drawing the chiseled line of his mouth into an upward curve that was like a caress.

"Oh, Christy," Natalie went on, refusing to be comforted, "I don't want you to go away from here—not ever! Now I wish dad hadn't taken me away to New York. If I'd been here I wouldn't have let you get married. Never, never, never!"

Joshua's thunderstruck eyes fastened on Christy's,

seeking denial. When he found none he went gray, as gray as he had looked that first day so long ago. Only this time the expression that gradually came over his mouth and into his eyes was terrible to see. He turned without a word and stalked to his own bedroom, a slamming door his only comment on what he had heard.

OLD TOM WAS COMMUNICATING with Christy now;
Joshua wasn't. Or, to be more exact, over the past few
weeks his conversation had become almost as mono-
syllabic as Old Tom's had once been. True, Joshua had
given Christy a briefing on the results of Natalie's
testing—but it had been a cold-faced interview, strictly
to the point and soon over. He had avoided looking at
her throughout.

The lie had been believed, and corroborated. Shortly
after Joshua's return from New York, a phone call had
come from the owners of the guesthouse, asking why no
visitor had shown up at their door. And then Old Tom,
learning of the supposed marriage, had told everyone of
his suspicions. With relief on his honest walnut face, he
had voiced his delight in discovering that Christy and
her "young feller" had been honeymooning all the
while. "Knew there was more to it than met the eye," he
said happily. "Ayeh. More than met the eye."

There had been congratulations from Mrs. Cousins,
who seemed genuinely delighted. "I'm only sorry I
didn't meet him, Christy," had been her sole complaint.
"But I'm sure he's a fine young man, or you wouldn't
have married him. What are your plans for the fall?"

"I don't know," Christy had answered, relieved that
for once she did not have to prevaricate. Europe, perhaps, she wondered to herself. A letter had come from
David, enclosing a check that she intended to cash.

David needed his pride more than he needed the money. But the letter caused another lie, for it had come addressed to her maiden name. "Habit," she had explained, and a laugh had covered that small white fib.

Life had become a giant lie. "Oh what a tangled web we weave...." Joshua had reminded her of that adage some time ago. Christy, now caught in the skein of her own deception, was learning that it was only too true.

The matter of the missing engagement ring had come up long ago, in Joshua's presence, at the dinner table. Natalie had spotted its absence on the second night after her return.

"What happened to your other ring, Christy? Did you give it back?"

"Not a bit of it, Natalie." Christy smiled at the purple eyes, hating herself all the while. She noted with some part of her mind that Joshua kept his glance averted, fixed on an imaginary spot on the tablecloth. "You see, a ring like that needs to have the setting checked once in a while, just to make sure the stones don't fall out. I took it into town, to the jeweler's on Main Street. With old rings like that you can't be too careful."

"That one looks old, too," Natalie observed. "Old and worn out."

"And so it is," answered Christy, "quite old."

"Why did he give you an old ring? Why not a new one?"

"Well...." Why did every question seem to lead to another lie? If Joshua had not been there, perhaps she would have been able to think of something to satisfy Natalie. But for the moment Christy's mind went blank, and it was Natalie herself who provided an answer— and a rescue.

"Is it because it belonged to his mother—like you said the other ring did?"

"Why, yes, Natalie, that's right. His mother's ring."

"It's kind of plain-looking, but I like it better than the other one," Natalie said with devastating honesty.

"Wedding rings are always plainer," Christy told her.

"Why?" persisted Natalie.

Christy thought for a minute. "I don't know, Natalie. I really don't."

Natalie turned to her father then, insistent upon satisfying her curiosity. "Why, dad?"

Joshua answered his daughter evenly enough, after a momentary pause. "Because a wedding ring is like a promise, Natalie. Promises are always plain, or they should be."

And Christy had known that although his eyes were directed to Natalie, his words were directed to her. It was as close as he had come, during these past weeks, to communicating his feelings about what had happened.

But now the lie did not have to be kept up so very much longer. Plans had been made for Natalie to enter a special school in September. And September was very nearly here . . . the summer virtually over, the lie almost lived out.

Vacation time had only one more week to go when Natalie remembered another promise—a promise Joshua had not yet kept. In Christy's presence she reminded her father one Sunday night at the evening meal.

"When are we going digging for quahogs, dad? You promised we would."

Joshua passed a hand over his jaw, thoughtfully. As usual, he directed his words and his eyes to Natalie in a way that did not include Christy. "Yes, I did. And a promise is a promise. We'll go tomorrow afternoon, if it doesn't rain."

"The weatherman promised it wouldn't," said Natalie.

Joshua gave a hollow laugh. "Well, that's one promise you can't count on. But let's hope he's right. In the morning you can hunt up the quahog rakes, Natalie. They should be in the garage. They're the ones with long strong teeth. We'll need two of them, and a couple of big pails."

"*Two* of them? You promised you'd take Christy, too."

"It doesn't matter," said Christy quickly. "I've gone digging for clams before. I don't have to go with you."

"You must! Quahogs aren't just any old clams," Natalie claimed in a superior way, then confessed more endearingly, "although I'm not sure why. What's different about them, dad?"

Joshua explained. "The shell is round and hard, much harder than an ordinary clam shell. And they're very difficult to open! You need a special knife, and if you don't twist it in exactly right, the shells have to be steamed open on the stove."

"That sounds hard."

"Maybe, but it's worth it. Quahog chowder is the best there is—the very best."

"I'll make the chowder, then," Christy offered, hoping that would keep Natalie from pursuing the matter of her participation in the hunt. "I know how. And tomorrow is Monday—Mrs. Cousins's day off."

"No, you have to come," Natalie said stubbornly. "Dad promised."

"But Christy didn't," Joshua pointed out, reasonably enough. "Maybe she doesn't want to come."

Natalie's face fell. "It's probably the last chance we'll have to do anything together, all of us. Please, Christy . . . please?"

And so, reluctantly, a new promise was made. The prospect of tomorrow's clamming filled Christy with dread, but it put Natalie into a state of great excitement.

"Why can't we go first thing in the morning?" she begged. "Please, dad?"

"I suppose that's possible," Joshua said, then caught himself. "Oh, no, the ring. I almost forgot about the ring."

"Ring? What ring?" asked Natalie. "Christy's ring?"

Joshua permitted himself a glance in Christy's direction. But he avoided her eyes; it was her ring finger that claimed his attention. "No, not Christy's ring. This is a ring they give you when you ask for a permit to dig quahogs. We can't keep any shells that are small enough to go through it. Those are seed quahogs and still growing. It's an iron ring; you couldn't use a . . . ." His voice trailed away and a peculiar look came over his lean features.

"What's the matter, dad?" prompted Natalie.

Joshua seemed visibly to shake himself back to the present moment. His eyes left Christy's hand and returned to Natalie. There was an odd timbre to his voice. "You couldn't use a wedding ring. It would never do. I'll have to go into town in the morning."

"Maybe there's a quahog ring in the garage," Natalie urged eagerly, "with the rakes."

"There's still the permit to think of," Joshua said slowly. His gray eyes were enigmatic now. "No, Natalie, you'll have to be patient. I'll have to go into town in the morning. Why don't you pack a picnic lunch tomorrow? I may be a bit late, but you could wait for me, couldn't you—you and Christy?"

"We'll wait," said Natalie happily.

And wait they did, for it was nearly two o'clock the next afternoon when Joshua finally returned from the town of Nantucket, and even Christy was becoming anxious for his return by the time the low-slung Mer-

cedes finally reappeared in the driveway. They all set
out without further ado, for Joshua had gone into town
casually clad in lean cream denim jeans and a cool
madras sports shirt, ready for the afternoon's clamming. His bathing suit was rolled in a towel in the tiny
back seat of the car. Rakes and buckets were thrown
into the same confined space, and Natalie scrunched in
beside them, for it was not a proper passenger seat.

Christy sat beside Joshua in the front. She had worn
her brown bikini under a thigh-length embroidered
smock of unbleached cotton, a choice she was now regretting, for in the confines of the car she felt overwhelmingly conscious of her long bare legs. True, they
were berry brown after the summer, and the smock
covered more than a bathing suit would. But the knowledge that Joshua's eyes kept traveling to the passenger
seat unnerved her, and she clasped her hands deter-
minedly over her knees in an effort to hide as much skin
as possible from his view.

"Can we go to Surfside?" Natalie asked over their
shoulders. "I like the breakers."

"No. We'll have to head for quiet waters," Joshua told
her. "Quahogs don't like the surf. But I know a good
private stretch of beach, and with luck we'll have it all
to ourselves. Did you remember to bring some old tennis shoes, Natalie?"

"I nearly forgot, but Christy reminded me." The tennis shoes were to protect the feet from sharp shells or
broken glass that might be raked up from the bottom.
"And did *you* remember the ring?"

"How could I forget?" asked Joshua lightly, in a way
that asked for no reply. And his next words might have
been in Christy's imagination, for they were no more than
a murmur through half-closed lips. "How indeed. . . ."

THE PICNIC LUNCH HAD BEEN DEMOLISHED; the clams had been dug. A whole bed of quahogs had been found, and all three buckets were more than half-full. Natalie wanted Joshua to start opening shells at once, but this he refused to do.

"Not now, Natalie! I need a rest. You go and use up some of that energy building a sand castle."

"If Christy helps me," Natalie said.

"Christy is not going to help you," returned Joshua firmly. "She's going to stay here and sit under the umbrella with me." All three had stripped to bathing suits now, although Joshua still wore a shirt over his, half-buttoned.

"No, I'd rather—" started Christy, but Joshua interrupted at once.

"You're staying here, Christy. I need to ask your advice about something. Run along, Natalie. And don't come back until I call you. Shoo!"

The tone of his voice was stern, and Natalie, recognizing it, obeyed with some reluctance, dragging her feet to the shoreline. Christy saved her comments until Natalie was out of earshot, for it seemed quite likely that Joshua wanted to talk about his daughter's forthcoming school season. She tried to keep her voice casual, but it was hard, for this was the first time she and Joshua had been alone since midsummer.

"Did you want to talk to me about Natalie?"

"And other things," said Joshua easily. "I really do want to get your opinion on something. Do you mind if I take my shirt off?"

"Not at all," said Christy, rigid in every limb.

Joshua loosened the remaining buttons of his shirt and shrugged it off completely. Christy kept her eyes to herself, but not her thoughts.

Joshua unfolded his spare frame and stretched out to his full extent, his torso on the oversize beach towel they shared, his legs on the sand.

"Relax, Christy," he said softly. "I won't bite you. You're a married woman, remember? Surely that's enough protection for you. There's no reason for awkwardness between us now. Lie down and take it easy while I talk to you."

She did so without relaxing, wishing that the two feet between them were in fact ten. For a moment she wondered if Joshua had suggested this because it meant they were half-hidden from Natalie's view by the rise of a sand dune and some spindly grass.

"You're safe with me now," Joshua said as if he had read her thoughts. "And for more than one reason. I've decided to get married myself, Christy."

Her fragile world shattered like a dropped Christmas ornament, exploding her careful defenses into a thousand fragments. *Married.* . . . Christy squeezed her eyes closed, and tears splintered behind the lids. *Married.* She hardly heard his next words for the dizzy reverberations in her ears and the clutching sickness in her stomach.

"I told you I might be able to make a decision like that after New York," Joshua was going on. "You advised me not to change my original plans for that week, Christy, and somewhere along the line I decided it was excellent advice."

So he had seen Doris in New York. Christy had been sick with wondering for weeks, and the confirmation was like another slap in the face. Yet what could she expect, when she herself had been willing to give him nothing?

"Frustration does terrible things to a man," Joshua was saying. "I told you it kept me from thinking straight. Well, I've made the decision now. I have to face the fact that I'm the marrying type. I realized while I was in New York that I wouldn't be getting married for Natalie's sake—I'd be getting married for my own sake. Well, Christy, aren't you going to congratulate me?"

"That's...very nice," she said in a faint voice. "I'm happy for you. Is it...anyone I know?"

"How did you guess?" he drawled, his eyes enigmatic as they rested on her mouth. "You may not be in accord with my choice, but I think she has the kind of...passion I need in a woman. Still, I have one thing left to decide, and that's where I want your help. You're a levelheaded, practical sort of person, Christy. Will you help me make up my mind? It has to do with how soon I get married."

"I don't think I can help with that," she managed to say. Her eyes remained closed, hurting behind the lids.

"Ah, but you can." Christy heard sounds of Joshua shifting on the towel and sensed that he had rolled onto his side to face her. "I have to decide whether to let the plastic surgeons finish their work before I get married...or after. I'm afraid my bride may be repelled by the way I look right now. What do you think?"

"Ask her," returned Christy in a strained voice. "I can't speak for another woman."

"She claims she isn't repelled," Joshua said pleasantly. "She claims to be attracted."

"Well, then." Christy made a deprecating gesture with one hand.

"How can I believe her? She refuses to look at my scars. Perhaps she's just being kind."

"Surely you can tell by her reaction." *Please, Joshua, stop this torture*, Christy's mind screamed.

"No, I can't. Oh, she seemed to forget the scars when I, ah, was with her, but perhaps that was just in the passion of the moment. The scars have faded a bit, but they're still ugly. How will she feel living with them day in, day out...sharing a bed with a man who looks like this? Touching him—"

Christy felt her wrist being grasped and drawn across the space between them, a gesture that forced her to turn slightly toward Joshua; then Joshua's hand pressing her hand against his chest. Ridges of scar tissue met her fingers...and beneath them, the hard ribs, the corded muscles, the feel of him that she had wanted to explore so many times.

"Please, Joshua, don't."

"Open your eyes, Christy." His voice was rough now, issuing a command. "I have to know how a woman reacts to this...this mess. I'm counting on you to tell the truth. Look at me. If you don't, I'll have to believe that my body really is repugnant to a woman."

And so her eyes came open. The scars were still ugly, as Joshua had said, but she had always known they were there, and in her mind's eye she had seen Joshua like this a thousand times. If anything she had expected worse. Time had healed the surrounding flesh, softening their impact, and the surface texture of his skin was as captivating to her as ever.

It was a moment before Christy realized that Joshua's hand was no longer holding hers in place. She started to withdraw her fingers, but he said in a low vibrant tone, "Don't stop now. Touch me, Christy."

It was as though she had been given permission to do the thing she had always wanted to do: to touch and touch and keep on touching. And so, with her senses in a whirlpool, she obeyed. Her fingers began to adventure over the hard sinewy warmth of his chest. And then there were two hands roaming, although she could not have said when her second hand joined the first. She was no longer touching only the scars, for in the swirl of sensuous feelings she had forgotten why her fingers were there. She quivered to feel the fine molding of his shoulders, the elastic hardness of his tendons, the lean corded flatness below his ribs. Compulsively she touched the shadowed cavity of his navel and saw his stomach muscles tense as he drew in his breath. And then, still in a trance, she was dragging a fingernail beneath the edge of his brief bathing suit. . . .

Oh, God, what was she doing? She snatched her hands and her eyes away. Joshua had asked for an opinion, not an examination. If she had communicated anything to him, it was only the knowledge that she was a wanton in her need for him—despite her wedding ring, despite his forthcoming marriage, despite everything. She raised one hand to her eyes, curtaining her face, and rolled away.

But if Joshua had noted her shamelessness, he made no comment on it. His tone remained conversational. "Well, Christy, what's the verdict? Shall I get married now or later?"

"You'll still have to ask her," Christy whispered through a hurting throat. "I'm afraid I can't help you."

"Too bad," Joshua said in an offhanded voice. "Ah, well . . . perhaps I'll put off the operations for now. Having made the decision to get married, I'm quite impatient. I need a woman to warm my bed, and not just any woman, and not just once in a while. Every night. That's the kind of man I am."

"Joshua, *please*—"

"Please what, Christy? I've never made a secret of the fact that I'm a man who needs a woman. I've had enough of separate bedrooms to last me for a lifetime."

"Spare me the intimate details."

"If you prefer." He rolled onto his back again and lay

content and silent for a time. White-bellied clouds sailed by in an unbelievably blue sky, and for Christy the moment became unbearable.

At last, unable to stand it any longer, she sat up and said, "Couldn't we go home now? I think I've had enough. . . ."

"Have you? Too bad—Natalie's having such a good time with her sand castle. Ah, well, toss me my trousers, will you?" He, too, came up to a sitting position. Then, as Christy reached for the cream denims and passed them over to him, he said nonchalantly, "Oh, by the way, Christy, when I was in town this morning I thought I'd do an errand for you. Something you forgot in town. . . . I've got it in my jeans." Without putting the denims on, he started to rummage through the pockets.

"Something I forgot?" She could remember nothing, but perhaps at this moment she was not thinking too clearly.

"Why, yes," he answered agreeably. "I thought I'd save you a trip, stop by and pick it up. Mind you, it was quite a hunt to find it. I looked over every ring that had been brought in all summer."

She stared at him, beyond speech at this moment. The engagement ring. Joshua was talking about David's engagement ring. And now he was pulling something small out of the pocket of his denims. Something small and gold and glowing with a warm yellow fire. And not so very small at all.

"It's an Oriental topaz, Christy, which is really a yellow sapphire. Suits you, don't you think? When I couldn't locate the other one, I knew you'd need this."

But she could not believe her eyes or her ears or the pounding of her heart. Or the fact that Joshua's hand had come to claim hers again; that he was removing the antique wedding band and replacing it with a ring of his own choice; that he was asking her to—

"Marry me, Christy," he said softly. The smile on his mouth and in his deep-set eyes was warm. Warm and loving, offering her everything she wanted...offering her more than she had dreamed possible. "Marry me at once. I've waited far too long already. Say yes, Christy, and put me out of my misery. A man can go mad with too much waiting."

She stumbled over her words and her thoughts. Questions tumbled out—questions and answers, all at once, breathless and confused. "But you said.... I don't understand.... Oh, yes, Joshua, yes, yes, *yes*! But how...?"

"Christy—" He stopped her babble of words in the best possible way, folding her into his arms and confirming his offer of marriage with a kiss that was gentle and searching, tender and tempestuous all at once. It was as well that Natalie still had her attention directed to the sand castle down by the water's edge.

Joshua soon pulled away, putting Christy firmly out of temptation's reach, but not before he murmured into her hair, "Sometimes it's hell being a father. You know what I'd do if we were alone, don't you?"

Christy was still breathless after his kiss, but now the questions came more rationally. Love and happiness spilled into her eyes.

"Oh, Joshua, how did you know?"

"It was the ring, Christy—that old gold wedding ring. It could never have been a partner to something made of platinum and diamonds. Yet you said it had belonged to David's mother. I realized you must have been lying. And if you lied about one thing, what was to stop you from lying about another? You trapped yourself in one untruth too many."

"But that was weeks ago. I thought you had accepted the lie long ago."

"I had, more's the pity. But I didn't really look at your wedding ring until yesterday. Then I knew I had to start checking on your story. Lies, lies, lies, Christy! Not one lie but many; it took me all morning to track them down. Oh, Christy, how could you put me through such torture?"

"You put me through some, too," she told him, but the expression on her face forgave him for all of it. "I would never have lied if I hadn't needed to defend myself against you—or perhaps just against yourself. I knew I couldn't keep saying no to an affair. And you told me that was all you wanted."

"I also told you I might be able to think straight after New York. And I *was* able to. I decided an affair wasn't the only thing I wanted."

And what had made him decide that, Christy wondered fleetingly. The end to his frustrations? But she pushed the nasty little cancer from her mind. She would never ask what had happened in New York. If a temporary liaison with Doris had made him decide on marriage, then perhaps she owed the other woman an enormous debt of gratitude.

"What other lies did you track down this morning?" she asked, forcing away visions of auburn hair fanned against a strong lean body.

"One thing led to another. First the ring. Then I checked into wedding licenses and found that none had been issued for you around that time. Of course that wasn't conclusive; you might have been married off Nantucket or obtained a license long ago. Next the taxi company. That was easy; there aren't a lot of taxis on this island. Last night I questioned Tom Maybee more closely about what he had seen and what he hadn't seen.

I knew he thought there had been a taxi, but there hadn't been. And your fiancé had to get to the airport somehow, didn't he? That brought the truth a little closer. And finally I confirmed everything with a phone call to Baltimore."

"You phoned *David*?" she asked with mingled alarm and surprise.

"Yes. And because I'm a doctor, I had no trouble getting through to him. I'm afraid he gave me an earful."

"Oh, Joshua...I'm sorry. I guess that means that David's still upset."

"As he very well should be—look what he lost! His pride took a beating. He told me in no uncertain terms what he thought of me for sleeping with you. It seems I'm not the only person you've been lying to."

Christy gave a half-embarrassed laugh. "Did you set him straight?"

"Why should I?" Joshua's eyes feathered into a smile that made Christy's flesh quiver with love. "It's an oversight I'm planning to correct as soon as possible. Now don't blush and look like that, or I may forget that my daughter is within shouting distance. *Our* daughter."

The reminder brought another thought to Christy, a nagging one. "I don't know what we'll tell Natalie. And Mrs. Cousins—and Old Tom."

"We could try the truth. I happen to be a great believer in it. Think of the trouble it could have saved us!" Joshua paused, then commented, "Do you think we can manage to base our marriage on truth from now on? I'd hate to think that lying might become a habit."

Christy laughed again, breathlessly. "It won't, I promise. I want nothing but trust between us."

He caught at her hand then, drawing it to his lips and planting a lingering kiss on her ring finger where the Oriental topaz cast its golden glow. "You really are a remarkable woman, Christy. Do you trust me so much already? I've been waiting for the question, and as it seems it's not forthcoming, I'll ask it for you. Aren't you curious about what happened in New York?"

"No," she answered truthfully. "I know all I want to know about New York. It made you decide to marry me, didn't it?"

"Oh, Christy, no wonder I love you," Joshua said in a disturbingly warm tone, and the contours of his mouth curved into a smile. "Well, if you won't ask, I'll tell you. My original plan—my very *first* plan—was to take you to New York and decide how I felt about things while we were there. I told you I'd taken your advice and stuck to my original plan, didn't I? At least as much as possible, considering you weren't with me. I made my decision on my first night there, and I would have told you so on the phone, but it's such an unfeeling instrument. I came back to Nantucket knowing you were the woman for me—the *only* woman for me. And I came back every bit as frustrated as when I went away. I still am."

Christy looked into his eyes and saw the truth and the need, and the love that went hand in hand with the need. A need she could now fill, wanted to fill.

"I promise to do something about that as soon as possible, Joshua," she said softly.

SHE KEPT HER PROMISE that same night, under a night sky strewn with trembling stars. When others were asleep and Natalie left in the care of Mrs. Cousins, they walked down to the moonlit stretch of Joshua's private beach and spread blankets on the warm sand and sealed their pact of love with the pale silent ghost of Graydunes hovering high in the distance.

Despite the months and years of frustration, Joshua

was patient in his impatience, schooling himself to be gentle. He undressed her with a slowness and tenderness that Christy found deeply touching, for she felt the passion quivering in his fingertips and saw the raw hunger in his moon-shadowed eyes and knew how hard it must be for him to go at her pace.

He kissed her ears and her throat and her breasts and told her of his love in ragged whispers. She heard the torment of waiting in his voice and reached for his buttons and his belt. She undressed him quickly, smoothing his clothes away with hands far more importunate than his. And when they lay naked together she reached and boldly stroked, telling him with pliant wanton fingers he did not have to wait.

He groaned and stopped her hand, putting it aside. "For mercy's sake, not now," he said in a cracked voice. "Not tonight."

Then he nudged her legs apart, and his fingers shook at the sweet warm feel of her as he gentled her thighs to receive him, but somehow he checked his haste. When he mounted her, he poised and took time to smooth her hips and caress her breasts and kiss her eyelids, and his breathing grew harsh and painfully erratic with the effort of holding his urgency.

But even after the first swift stroke when he made her his, he grew still, helping her through the moment with a deep and passionately tender kiss.

She felt the terrible need in him, the fierce shuddering that traveled in great strong rivers through his rigid shoulder muscles as he attempted to control himself. She felt the tight shaking tension of his corded thighs, the powerful pulsing containment that must be aching for release.

With stroking fingers and giving lips and sensuously stirring hips she encouraged him to take his pleasure at once. In the taking there would be giving, and already her flesh was flushed and feverish with the need to discover the full meaning of her womanhood.

With mouths hungrily clinging, with arms wound around each other, with limbs grown swiftly hectic, they reached for the beautiful rhythms of passion. And together, in a soaring burst of shared ecstasy, they found the wild, wondrous, shuddering culmination of their love.

When her arching hips had grown still beneath Joshua's sprawled and spent body, Christy stroked slow fingers over the moon-silvered head bent into her throat. "I love you, Joshua," she murmured, repeating the simple words that seemed so wonderfully new with each saying. "I love you so very, very much."

He lifted his head and looked down at her with dark shadowed eyes, his expression somber and deeply tender. "And I love you—Mrs. Brent."

"Not yet," she reminded him softly.

He pecked a line of small kisses along her jaw. "Very soon," he murmured. He buried his face in her hair, drinking deeply of its fragrance. "We'll marry as soon as possible—although nothing's quite soon enough for me. All this should have happened weeks ago. Oh, God, how I love you. . . ."

And they spent some sweet moments whispering about the marvels of each other's bodies, about the magic of each other's embraces, about the wonderments of each other's love.

Soon Joshua shifted his lean body, levering his weight away to lie alongside Christy on the blanket. With his hands he began to stroke softly, in slow praise of the long, smooth, womanly curves of her lying gilded in the moonlight. "Tomorrow night I intend to go very slowly with you," he muttered. "Very slowly indeed."

She could hear the slight roughening of his voice, could feel the tremble returning to his fingers. In moments he drew his hands away and rolled onto his back, and she knew he was trying not to overwhelm her on the first night.

Christy smiled a small secret smile to herself, deciding it would soon be time for her to grow bold. Joshua had a lot of catching up to do.

She raised herself on one arm and hovered over him, looking warmly down into his darkened eyes. Slowly and provocatively she teased his chest with the tips of her seductively stirring breasts, loving the muscular male feel of him beneath her, loving the sudden tensing of his taut stomach muscles, loving the low groan that sounded in his throat.

"Joshua," she murmured as her fingers began to travel, "I know you're probably tired, but I have this strange temptation. . . ."